UNTIL DAWN TOMORROW

Birmingham cop Detective Inspector Frank Kavanagh is pursuing a murderer who may have killed several times . . . but he is prey to a growing feeling that he 'knows' the man he is looking for.

In his search for the killer Kavanagh becomes increasingly disturbed by his own aggressive impulses. Gradually he pieces together a dark history of infidelity and deceit, and an obsessive personality emerges. For Kavanagh, though, the final confrontation is as much with his inner self as with the murderer.

David Armstrong's new book is a brooding psychological murder mystery which moves from the Midlands to a chilling climax in the urban nightmare of London. As gripping and original as his highly praised debut novel, *Night's Black Agents*.

UNTIL DAWN
TOMORROW

David Armstrong

HarperCollins*Publishers*

Collins Crime
An imprint of HarperCollins*Publishers*
77−85 Fulham Palace Road, London W6 8JB

First published in Great Britain
in 1995 by Collins Crime

1 3 5 7 9 10 8 6 4 2

© David Armstrong 1995

The Author asserts the moral right to be
identified as the author of this work

A catalogue record for this book is
available from the British Library

ISBN 0 00 232552 7

Set in Meridien and Bodoni

Photoset by Rowland Phototypesetting Ltd
Bury St Edmunds, Suffolk
Printed and bound in Great Britain by
HarperCollinsManufacturing Glasgow

For Elizabeth Walter

1

'Good morning, Inspector. Still raining?' Dr Khaliq, entombed in his subterranean mortuary, perennially inquired of his callers what the weather was like outside. This mattered less to policemen and officials, whose business was conducted with a certain professional detachment, than to distraught relatives who, summoned by the authorities to identify a corpse, and bracing themselves for the ordeal ahead, were often discomfited to find the doctor more interested in the meteorological than the frequently charged emotional climate.

'Drizzling a bit, I think,' replied Kavanagh as he approached the body on the marble slab.

'Umm,' said Khaliq, clearly disappointed by the nebulousness of the policeman's weather report. He continued his scrubbing down and called over his shoulder, 'What do you know about him?'

'Art teacher. Worked at the local college.' Kavanagh turned back the sheet a foot and stared at the drained face. He avoided the eyes. Khaliq came to the other side of the slab, drying his hands.

The inspector was aware of the pathologist's gaze upon him. It was a challenge. Kavanagh ceded the point and looked at the dead man's eyes. He nodded his head a fraction. The doctor drew back the sheet another three feet.

Kavanagh looked at his manhood. The corpse was a painting by Lucien Freud: pallid flesh, dead pubic hair;

the penis, shrunk to the size of a woman's finger; the testicles, one larger than the other, lying to one side of the inner thighs, the dark brown scrotum of creased and folded skin.

Khaliq raised an eyebrow. Kavanagh sensed the flicker of movement on the pathologist's brow and looked up to the wounds.

They were very 'clean', surgically deep. The first through the lower ribcage and into the heart. The other, just above it, perhaps two or three inches. There was no 'tearing', and the wounds, though very close, had remained separate.

Many murderers, following the convention of countless plays and films, shot or stabbed people in the place where they *assumed* the heart to be, only to find their victims giving evidence against them ten or twelve months later. The heart was much more central in the torso than many would-be killers appeared to realize. But the person who had stabbed art teacher John Lacey to death appeared to know his basic anatomy.

'What can you tell us?' asked Kavanagh without looking up from the corpse. The doctor exhaled a long breath which blew faintly off the dead man's body and brushed Kavanagh's face. The policeman recoiled from the intimacy of the contact.

Khaliq reiterated the essence of what he had spoken into his dictaphone an hour ago: 'He has been stabbed to death with a long, sharp blade. Two wounds. The first, here,' Khaliq put his finger half an inch from the upper incision, 'this wound punctured the pulmonary artery. The second wound' – he moved his finger slightly down the chest – 'into the right atrium was redundant. The haemorrhage from the artery was massive and would have meant death in three or four minutes.'

The policeman asked neutrally, 'Was he gay?'

Khaliq, a highly educated man, whose father had come

to this country from Srinagar forty years ago, had a marked antipathy towards stereotyping. 'Not very "politically correct", is it, Inspector?' And he added peevishly, 'Just because he's an art teacher, he doesn't *have* to be gay, does he?'

'Just a thought,' said Kavanagh. 'And being "politically correct" won't get some knife-wielding maniac off the streets and into the dock. I like to start with the obvious, move on to the wacky, then get the shrinks, psychics, water diviners and mystics in . . .'

'And when all that fails?' said the doctor. Meteorologist Khaliq regarded his policemen colleagues as a necessary inconvenience: inexact, shuffling people who brought him his raw material, but always returned, usually in the middle of the weather forecast, with their bad clothes, detectable body odours, irritating habits and foolish quips.

Kavanagh ignored him. 'So, was he gay?'

The doctor glanced up at Kavanagh. 'I don't think so. His sphincter has no obvious tearing or bruising, the anal muscles aren't slack. They're about right for a mid-forties male. Do you want to have a look?'

'No thanks. I'll take your word for it,' said Kavanagh.

'It's not conclusive, of course,' added Khaliq. 'These days, lots of homosexuals, the sensible ones anyway, they don't penetrate. Is he married?'

'Yes.'

'Children?'

Kavanagh looked at the face again. 'Yes, a son.' The man's beard had continued to grow in the few hours since his murder. He had a strong, dark stubble. He had been a good-looking man, handsome really, with strong features. But there was something neanderthal about the jaw. A suggestion of something that the policeman had seen in encyclopaedias on primitive man, the sort of thing that cartoonists pick up and accentuate in a deft line that makes that one feature the essence of their subject.

*   *   *

Kavanagh met Sergeant Presley as he walked into the third-floor incident room of the city-centre police station. 'How d'you get on down the body shop?' asked the insouciant sergeant.

'Nothing much; no revelations. Stabbed twice. Long, sharp blade. Deep cuts, straight through the heart.' There was a pause as Kavanagh actually thought of the corpse. A man of his own age.

Presley respected the moment's silence, and then asked, more considerately, 'What do you think?'

'Fuck knows,' said the DI, exasperated. He had seen it all before; knew that he would see it all again, and again. The sorrow, the grief, the pity, the terrible waste of it all. 'It's not a straightforward though.'

Kavanagh paused and mimicked a blade in his hand. At chest height he pushed it slowly through the giving air. A constable looked up and watched, intrigued, as the inspector went through his mime in the busy room. The brief piece of ham theatre over, the girl looked back to the word-processor screen and resumed her tapping of the keys.

Presley followed his boss to the coffee machine in the corner. The senior policeman continued, thinking aloud, 'The wounding's too . . . clinical. Whoever did it *knew* what he was doing. And he got close in.'

'He?' said Presley.

'Could've been a her, but I'd guess it was a bloke.'

'What do you mean, "Knew what he was doing"?'

'I dunno,' said Kavanagh. 'It doesn't look frenzied or wild. It's like an execution. And yet, whatever the poor bugger had done to "deserve" it, pros don't stab people when they want them topped. It's not a method they use, not here in Brum, any road.'

He sauntered away from the vending machine to his crowded desk. Presley picked up the muddy drink in its plastic cup and carried it to his boss.

2

At the parish centre in the churchyard of the Birmingham suburb where John Lacey had died, the scene-of-crime officers were going about their painstaking business. The whole area had been taped off, from the incongruous glass-and-concrete building that had been built from the parishioners' donations in the early 1970s, to the van that Lacey had been loading with his students' work when he had been stabbed to death the previous evening.

There was no sign of rain but, following textbook procedure, a blue plastic tent had been erected over the Toyota van and the place where the man had collapsed, bleeding, to his terrible death.

A uniformed officer lifted the tape as Kavanagh and Presley approached. Several people were gathered at the flimsy barrier. They had witnessed this scene a hundred times on television and at the cinema, and now, courtesy of John Lacey, art teacher at the local college, just as Andy Warhol had famously promised them, *their* fifteen minutes of sordid fame had finally arrived.

There was a theatrical hush amongst the expectant little crowd but also, undeniably, and rippling just beneath the surface, there was a feeling of bonhomie: the two dozen people standing there, united by this remarkable tragedy, were also bound by the smug knowledge that no matter how deep the furrows on their brows, or how gravely concerned were the looks on their faces, they were, finally, entirely untouched by this patent horror.

11

It was, in reality, better than the glimpsed spectacle of a motorway car crash: that was momentary, a fleeting gawp as the censorious traffic policeman hurried you off down the road. Here, like extras on a film set, there was ample time for discussion and speculation as the crowd waited patiently for the principals to make their entrances. No one had yet brought a shooting stick or a picnic stool, but one elderly man had thoughtfully provided himself and his wife with a flask of milky tea.

Inside the awning, Kavanagh and Presley stepped into plastic galoshes and pulled on disposable overalls and surgical gloves.

At the rear of the van, chalk marks on the ground indicated the position where the man had fallen. The scene looked uncannily like the cover of a cheap sixties paperback.

The two men crouched down near the chalk outlines while a young lady from forensic brushed dust and grit, moss and hair and fibres, from the ground into numbered plastic wallets. Her colleague carefully labelled each one.

Murder, reflected Kavanagh, not for the first time, was *so* time consuming. Terrible, yes, but also so *terribly* expensive. Like a blue whale cruising the southern oceans, its mouth agape, and swallowing its life-sustaining krill by the lorry load, so the beleaguered police force ate up billions and billions of pounds each year as crime detection, in reply to ever-more ingenious criminals, had to become more efficient.

True, most burglaries were never solved, and the stolen cars that *were* recovered were no longer worth having, but only seven per cent of murders had remained unsolved during the last decade.

This, of course, had little to do with sharp-eyed coppers, or the presence on the street of the public's beloved uniformed officers, but everything to do with electron microscopes, machines that could magnify a strand of cotton to the size of a tree trunk; DNA testing that could identify the blood or saliva or semen of a suspect to within a one in seven million margin of error; image enhancement and reconstruction techniques that could identify decomposed victims from the scantiest remains.

But all of this cost money: piles and piles of it. Everything by the book, everything in triplicate, everything on tape or video or film. It cost an absolute fortune.

Before Lacey had fallen, splashes of blood had hit the ground and exploded into a series of ever-larger blots on the paving slabs. They ended in a huge, dark red stain where the man's life had finally gushed out of him.

Kavanagh got to his feet and looked into the Toyota's open door. There were several canvases stacked inside the van ready to be tied into position. The man had, apparently, just taken one to the vehicle, and was on his way back into the building when the killer had struck.

Inside the parish centre, a female churchwarden was sitting in the kitchen with a policewoman. The two women drank tea from green, Beryl china cups and Miss Nicholson, her free hand lying demurely in her lap, prayed silently for the soul of the man whose violent death had led to the solemn industry that now surrounded the holy place.

She was a slim, fair-skinned woman in her late forties. She had told her story to the policemen the previous night, but had been distraught; they needed to hear it again.

A pianist who taught the suburb's promising youngsters and gave local recitals, Miss Nicholson knew about the moment's silence that should precede any performance.

When she 'had the floor', and knew that no more throats would be cleared or cups scraped on saucers by her audience of three, she focused her attention and began her reprise.

It had been dark. As arranged, after piano practice, at about 7.30, John Lacey, whom she knew a little, had come to collect the exhibition of his students' work which the centre had had on display for the last three weeks. 'It's

13

all part of the college's policy of going out into the wider community,' she patiently explained to the two men.

She had already taken down the paintings and was wrapping them in bubble foam for their short journey to the college. Lacey was carrying them out to the van.

She heard nothing unusual. After perhaps his third or fourth trip, he seemed to be gone rather a long time. She called to him, 'John, would you like a cup of coffee?'

There was no answer. She assumed, embarrassed, that he might have gone to the lavatory in the foyer. She remembered singing quietly to cover the awkwardness, and began to wrap another painting.

The silence continued too long, and the quiet in the building was uncanny. She listened for any sound, of water pipes or the cistern's filling.

She called his name again, this time from just inside the doorway of the meeting room where the paintings had hung. It was so quiet she could hear the fluorescent tubes humming. Suddenly she became afraid. She felt alone in the place and irrationally but terribly afraid.

She ran through the foyer and out of the front entrance. His body was lying beside the rear door of the van. She screamed. There was blood all around him. She was afraid for herself. She screamed again and again. She knelt down by the man, but was too frightened to touch him. She thought he was dead. 'I just screamed and screamed.'

And now it was time for *her* confession. She faltered, ashamed, 'I was afraid to touch him. I didn't know what to do. His face looked dreadful. In agony. He was wearing a blue denim shirt, but it was soaked dark red. I didn't know how to help. I'm sure he was dead.'

This was her fear. That she could have helped, done something, anything. And she knew she had done nothing for him. The constable laid her hand over the pianist's long fingers and said quietly, 'It's all right. You had a terrible experience. No one could have done any more.'

Miss Nicholson began again: 'Someone came running.

14

It was a young couple. The boy was first, but all he said was "My God! Oh, my God!". He must have thought that *I* had killed him. It never occurred to me.' She smothered a little mirthless laugh. 'The girl ran down the road and called an ambulance. The boy stood beside me, watching. I suppose he thought that I might try and kill him, too.' She reflected for a moment, lost in her own thoughts.

'Yes?' said Kavanagh quietly.

'Yes,' she repeated. 'Eventually he seemed to understand, and he brought me back in here. He put the kettle on.' She looked at the constable whose hand still covered hers. 'He used the hot water tap.'

The men looked at one another; the constable smiled.

'I didn't say anything.' She glanced at Presley. 'You shouldn't use the hot. Not for drinking. It's not *direct*, you see.'

'No, quite,' said Kavanagh.

3

The next morning, Kavanagh and Presley waited for ten minutes in Aidan McEwan's office at the sixth form college while the Scotsman spoke to his vice-principal in the adjoining room.

On the wall, behind his half-snooker-table-size desk was something called a Mission Statement. It had nothing to do with astronauts or space research, but was seven or eight lines of non-speak that ended with the phrase: *Osborne College: in training since 1936.*

'They should be ready soon!' said Presley.

Kavanagh inspected the titles on the bookshelves on the far side of the room. Most of them were American, and every author had the mandatory initial juxtaposed between fore- and surname: James C. Coady's *Motivating Managers*; Robert M. Grant's *Organizational Behaviour; Success: The Impossible Dream?*; and the pithily titled: *Talking to People who Listen, Speaking to People who Need to Hear.*

These books were clearly little short of apocalyptic, and the last one on the shelf, a huge tome called *101 Great Mission Statements*, was a work of such erudition that it had required not one, but two, editors to bring it to the notice of a mission-statement-hungry world.

Kavanagh was a policeman whose business was criminology and detection, and who knew a bit about forensic science. But they weren't the only books on his shelves. There were also a few novels, and some poetry, and a much-loved, ten-volume collected Shakespeare.

After all, everyone needs something. For some people it's hang-gliding, others build plastic models or collect stamps; some people do the garden, even read books on it. It all adds up.

But who was Aidan McEwan? A man with a 'mission statement' behind his desk, and pictures on his wall of Michael Edwardes and Ian McGregor, Margaret Thatcher's erstwhile industrial kneecappers.

When, finally, Aidan McEwan did come through the door into his office, he walked up to Kavanagh, stood very close and, without speaking, shook him solemnly by the hand.

'Gentlemen,' he said, nodding to Presley.

The men waited, but that *was* the sentence.

'Mr McEwan,' said Kavanagh.

'Terrible news,' offered the college principal. 'Terrible.'

'Yes, sir. Dreadful,' said Presley superfluously.

'Please, sit,' said McEwan, as he arranged himself behind his desk and settled himself into his high-backed, black chair.

'Coffee?'

The policemen declined.

'Please,' said the principal. 'Do begin.'

'We need background,' said Kavanagh. 'Anything at all on John Lacey. Any enemies. Was there anything that you were aware of: jealousies; rivalries; student problems; anything at all?'

McEwan leaned back in his chair, put the tips of his fingers together and, with the triangle formed there, put it to his lips. He eventually took them away, as if about to speak, looked from Presley to Kavanagh and back again, but said nothing.

Presley wondered if he had forgotten the question, was about to restate it in a slightly amended form, when the principal began.

'Education, gentlemen. Not what it was. Changes.

17

Significant. Sweeping. Not *all* welcome. Disruption, there is bound to be. Problems: no. Challenges: yes.'

This verbal equivalent of using the highlighting pen was not something that either of the policemen had encountered previously, and they sat fascinated but unsure of what exactly the principal was trying to say.

Eventually, when the man paused, Kavanagh said, 'And . . . Lacey? John Lacey? Did he have . . . "problems"?' ('Challenges' hardly seemed the appropriate word for the murdered man, even allowing for the unbridled optimism of Osborne College and its porcine principal.)

'None whatsoever,' said McEwan conclusively. 'None at all.' And he passed Lacey's personal folder across the wide desk to Kavanagh who, sitting in an easy chair, was a foot below him.

'I've been through it this morning. Nothing.'

Generally speaking, people did not include in their CVs the reasons for their being murdered. Minutes of meetings never gave the cut and thrust, the real story beneath the carefully chosen and recorded words.

Notwithstanding McEwan's apparently unshakeable faith in the contents of Lacey's buff folder, the policemen continued to ask questions about the deceased art teacher for another thirty minutes or so.

The principal answered in his idiosyncratic manner. But he was a man used to setting agendas, not following those of others and, at the slightest opportunity, he relapsed into his generalized educational patois of cliché and euphemism: thus, college students had metamorphosed into 'clients'; things that were being developed were 'on-line'; suggestions were 'proactive'.

There was a tired, third-hand quality about his discourse. He was a man who spent his days 'moving the goalposts'; and looking for 'level playing fields'; for he had, apparently single-handedly, 'a lot of balls to keep in the air'.

Kavanagh grew weary. He was desperate to escape the

aural, watery clasp of this man who had taken on the management equivalent of the sign that used to hang in every two-bit, one-telephone office in the land: *You don't have to be mad to work here, but if you are it helps.*

Eventually, Kavanagh and Presley thanked the principal for his time and backed away towards the door.

But he was now in full flow, escorting them down the corridors, and out to their Granada, calling after them in the car park, 'Education. It'll never be the same again, you know,' and finally offered triumphantly, 'Our people, they deliver the curriculum on Sunday after*noons.'*

Presley drove away, throwing the back end of the car into the air as he ignored the speed humps.

So, rubicund Aidan McEwan was the sort of man into whose care the education and nurturing of the country's young had now been placed. For the first time since he had been called in to investigate the art teacher's death, Inspector Frank Kavanagh found a crumb of comfort in the tragedy.

4

It was a detached house: 1930s; four bedrooms; double garage and a big front garden with a couple of birch saplings and some ornamental fruit trees with lots of late-season pink blossom on them. Kavanagh had given up trying to make sense of it any more: there were daffodils at Christmas, and strawberries in the shops in November. No wonder the prisons were full.

Presley pulled their black Ford onto the tarmac drive and stalled it by taking his foot sharply off the clutch while keeping his other firmly on the brake.

Kavanagh looked at him disapprovingly. Why not just turn off the ignition key like everyone else? He *had* mentioned it. Often.

The garage up-and-over doors were open and there was a restored maroon Morris 1000 Traveller there, a couple of well-used mountain bikes, plus strimmers and mowers and shears and extension leads. The tins of paint and primer and creosote and motor oil were neatly stacked on wide shelves beneath a big, very solid workbench.

The only things which distinguished this garage from thousands like it were the couple of painter's easels leaning against the breeze blocks, the very many paintings which were stacked against all three walls, and the tailor's dummy, propped at a crazy angle in the corner next to the aluminium stepladders.

The front door opened before they had rung the bell.

20

A teenager wearing a blue baseball cap bearing the white insignia of New York held it ajar.

'Inspector Kavanagh; Sergeant Presley. Hello, son. Can we come in?'

The boy opened the door a little wider, and the two men stepped along the parquet-floored hall into the front room.

Judith Lacey was tall, five feet eight or nine, and wore soft blue leather shoes that looked handmade. She was wearing a dress made of that crinkly material Kavanagh knew but couldn't remember the name of. The skirt hugged her slight tummy and came down to above her ankles. It was dark blue with little white flowers and was buttoned from the neck to the midriff.

The room was sparsely furnished, with two big Habitat linen sofas, some expensive Linn hi-fi separates, a slim-line television, lots of books on the shelves, stacks of records and CDs and tapes, and a couple of matt and stainless-steel occasional tables.

The only incongruity, blot on the glossy-magazine appearance of the room, were the three ashtrays, all big, French-café copies, the names Ricard and Pernod picked out on their distinctive yellow sides, but with several crushed cigarette ends in each.

'Mrs Lacey, I'm sorry to call again so soon. We have to ask you just a few more questions.'

She acknowledged his request with a barely perceptible inclination of her head.

She sat in the corner of the huge sofa, Kavanagh sat opposite her, forward on the chair, his hands hanging between his open knees. Presley stood at the window.

'An incident like this, we have to make our inquiries as soon as possible.' The inspector cringed at his use of the word 'incident'. The 'incident' here was the death of her husband. The man to whom she had been married for twenty years.

'I'm sorry.' It was a general apology, for his crassness,

for his use of the word, and for even being here again. 'The pathologist's examination, I understand it is completed?' The question was rhetorical; he knew that the body had been released into her keeping and was at the funeral parlour.

'Yes,' she murmured.

'And the funeral?'

'On Monday. Two-thirty, at Saint Jude's.'

'I would like to attend, if I may. And my sergeant.'

'Of course,' she said.

'We will be discreet.'

'I'm sure. Thank you.'

Her son pushed open the door and brought in a tray with cups and milk and sugar on it. His mother gave him a little smile of thanks. When he had returned with the Bodum of dark coffee and left, Kavanagh began. 'Have you thought of anything, anything at all, no matter how insignificant it might appear to you, which might give us a clue as to why anyone would want to . . . ?' His question trailed away.

'Frankly, Mrs Lacey, we're struggling. We've very little to go on. Anything you can suggest could be of enormous help.'

She lit a Silk Cut cigarette, exhaled the smoke as she began. 'The students he taught, they loved him. Lots of them kept in touch, after they'd gone off to college and things. He was very popular. People don't get killed . . . for no reason. Drugs, money, robberies. Yes, I know, the world we live in, but not this, for no reason, no reason . . .' and she broke down and began to sob.

Presley, who often spent Saturday afternoons bruising in the scrum for the Birmingham Police second fifteen, stood above her and put his hand lightly on her shoulder.

She regained some control and, embarrassed for the big policeman standing awkwardly at her side, unable to comfort her, unable to move from her side, mouthed a quiet 'Thank you'.

'This is all a nightmare. I can't believe what has happened. I don't want to "come to terms" with it. Be like those people on television who say that "life must go on". I don't *want* life to go on.

'The doctor has given me pills, but I don't want to take them. I want to feel this. This pain. My husband has gone. I don't want to not feel his loss. We went to the cinema last weekend. Last Sunday, he brought the tea up. Then made the breakfast, just like always on Sundays. Today, he's not here any more. I don't *want* to forget.'

Her words made the notion of the inspector's questions entirely redundant. Yes, he knew: she taught drama, but this was no performance, or if it was, she should be in Hollywood, not Sutton Coldfield.

Presley stepped away from her and poured the coffee.

Kavanagh knew that he had to do it, but he felt a cheat, a cheapskate. 'Your husband, John. His relationship with the teacher-training student . . . ?'

'Yes?'

'You told us yesterday that that was a difficult time for you. A very difficult time.'

'Yes. Of course.'

'How long did it go on for?'

'I don't know. Not long. She was on a placement. But it didn't start straightaway. Two, perhaps three weeks, I suppose.'

'And then you found out?'

'Yes.'

'Then what? I'm sorry, we *have* to know.'

'Then she went back to her college. It was all over.'

'You came to terms with it?'

'Eventually. It was difficult. We had been married nine or ten years. Perhaps we'd let things drift. Relationships, I think they have to be nurtured. Fed. Perhaps we had begun to take ours for granted. Are you married, Inspector?'

'No, I'm separated,' he replied.

'I see.'

Kavanagh had been forced to acknowledge that there didn't seem to be an appropriate response to the statement that you were 'separated'. It wasn't like saying your wife had died, when people might pause before saying, 'I'm so sorry.'

But he was aware that the timbre of his voice, even in uttering the apparently neutral words, failed to conceal his feelings of loss.

She began again, and said, perhaps a little too defensively, 'It wasn't a love affair. It was a brief infatuation.'

'How did you find out about it?' asked Presley gently.

She smiled. 'It's not funny. Not at all. I went to my mother's. My father hadn't been well. I often used to go there overnight. They live in the Malvern Hills, near Worcester. It's not far. I took Joe, of course.

'The next day, when we came back, I was in the bathroom. John's flannel was over the rim of the bath. There was something odd about it. I reached out and touched it. It was like cardboard. Completely dry. He hadn't been in the bathroom that morning.

'I just knew. You always do.' She glanced at Kavanagh. 'I was on my knees. Joe's watching cartoons on the TV downstairs, and I'm on my knees on the tiles on the bathroom floor, John's flannel, stiff as a board over the rim of the bath, telling me he's having an affair as clearly as if he'd left me a note on the mantelpiece.

'There were a hundred questions racing through my mind: Who was it? How long? Where? When? All the usual, grisly, horrible stuff.

'I just couldn't cope. You come up with all sorts of bizarre ideas. The truth's actually better than not knowing. I wanted to go down to college that very minute and ask him to tell me.'

'And?'

'I waited. That evening, he told me. I think he'd actually

given up on her, satisfied his little yearning, but she was still involved.'

She smiled again, this time had almost to stifle a little laugh. 'We formed an alliance against her. Me and John against *his* affair. There was a sort of grim humour about the whole thing. He didn't want any scandal at college, of course. It was just a question of getting through the next couple of weeks, and then her going back to her college.'

'And that was it?'

'Yes, that was it.'

'You were very supportive, Mrs Lacey,' said Presley. 'Not everyone would have been so.'

'Yes. But it was self-serving, really. After the shock, and the initial tears and upset, I knew that I didn't want us to break up. I knew that he didn't love her, or anything like that. So it was a sort of pragmatism.'

'And you got through?'

'What does Brecht say?'

Presley looked to Kavanagh. His look asked: 'What *does* Brecht say?'

'"Whatever doesn't kill me, makes me strong." We were stronger for it, I suppose.'

'Didn't you feel a need for revenge?' asked Kavanagh.

'Revenge?' she said.

'Perhaps an affair of your own? To "settle the score"? People do, you know,' he added, conciliatory.

'Everyone's entitled to a mistake, aren't they?' she rejoined. 'No, I didn't want revenge. I wanted us to be happy, a family, and together again. That's all. Why are you asking me about these things now?' she said.

Kavanagh saw no point in subterfuge. 'If you had seen the need . . . wanted to have a relationship . . . this could have led to . . . at the very least, there would have been motives.'

'For me to take John's life?' she said.

'Not necessarily you, Mrs Lacey,' added Presley.

'Oh, *my* jealous lover!' she said with mock scorn.

'It does happen,' said Kavanagh, defensive about the suggestion, notwithstanding his lack of belief in it. And for emphasis, 'It wouldn't be the first time.'

'Of course,' she offered politely. 'I have no lover, Inspector. I've never had one. I have no idea why someone has taken my husband's life, and ruined mine, and our son's.'

While Kavanagh went upstairs to the lavatory, Presley, who barely knew a dandelion from a radish, stood at the window and made a valiant attempt at horticultural small talk with the bereaved woman.

As he dried his hands, Kavanagh looked down at the three flannels that lay over the rim of the bath. The bottle-green one, slightly apart from the others, was bone dry.

'What do you reckon?' asked Presley as they drove away. There was an objective detachment about them now that they were away from the widow's claustrophobic grief. They might have been discussing a film they had just seen.

'There's always someone with half a reason to do someone in,' said Kavanagh, 'but usually it stops at half a reason. The moment passes. It's like on the motorway. You pass a hundred thousand drivers on the M1. Every one of them, all their brains ticking, their periods menstruating, their passions throbbing, their cats dying, their mothers ill. They all make all those split-second seventy- and eighty- and ninety-mile-an-hour decisions just right. And everyone gets home. But when just one of them makes a tiny error . . . I'm surprised there aren't *more*, not *less*.'

'Crashes?' said Presley, his eyes on the road.

'Murders,' said Kavanagh.

'So, what do you reckon?'

'God knows,' said Kavanagh.

5

The next day, on the Saturday afternoon, DI Frank Kavanagh convened a meeting of the dozen detectives who had been working nonstop on the Lacey murder inquiry.

The football results were coming in on the huge old Sony in the corner of the musty social club on the fifth floor. As they stuttered across the teleprinter, Bob Wilson, the John Major of the BBC's team of football pundits, reiterated the results with his customary lack of panache.

Manchester United had won again, beating Tottenham 2–1 at home, and had started to draw away from the following pack. There was already absurdly premature talk of them doing the double (the FA Cup had not yet even begun for the league clubs), possibly even the treble.

Kavanagh stood at the front of the room, his head slightly bowed, oblivious to the results and the background hubbub and banter. Presley reached up and turned off the set. DC Andy Reeder, originally from a bleak North Wales village, groaned as the screen went blank on the tantalizingly grim news: Brentford 2; Wrexham . . .

The inspector took a pace towards the big flip charts and began without ceremony. 'I'll state the obvious, go over what you all know. Anything you want to pick up on, stop me. John Lacey was forty-six. Taught art at the Osborne Sixth Form College. He'd been there eighteen years. Popular with the kids. The odd run-in with a student, but generally well liked. Popular in the staff room, too. Lots of friends. No particular enemies that we're aware of. No professional jealousies that we've been able to turn up.

'About ten years ago he had an affair with a student teacher who was attached to his department. It was a brief, passionate thing. His wife found out, they had a rocky time for a bit, and then the student left to go back to college and, as far as we know, they haven't seen each other since.

'The girl's been interviewed; she's married herself now, lives in York, a teacher. Her boyfriend at the time never knew about her affair, so she says. She looks above board. We're going to have to trace the boyfriend; he's emigrated to Canada, but it's probably a long shot. I think she's telling us the truth, and anyway, why's her ex-boyfriend going to come back and kill her one-time lover ten years later?

'Lacey's wife, Judith, told us about the affair. The way she tells it, she was upset at the time, but they got over it and, as far as we can find out, there was nothing going on in that area.'

Kavanagh pushed his fingers through his thick, dark hair. It was greasy, needed washing. 'Like a lot of art teachers, according to his wife, Lacey wanted to be a painter, was probably frustrated in that sense. But that doesn't seem to lead anywhere. He found time to do a bit of his own work, had an exhibition last year, which didn't set the world on fire.

'Background: working class, born here in Brum; first one of his generation to go to college; got his degree, got married (his wife teaches drama). He taught at Aldridge Road Comprehensive in north Birmingham for a couple of years, and then did a post-graduate something or other in South Wales.

'Came back up here, got the job at Osborne Tech, as it was then. A few years later they have a nipper, Joe. He works at the sixth form college for eighteen years and last Wednesday evening, October 13th, taking down an exhibition of his second-year students' work in the parish centre, someone walks up and stabs him to death. Any questions?'

Detective Sergeant Jackson raised his hand. Kavanagh nodded.

'What about his missis?'

'What about her?' said Kavanagh.

'What if she was playing away? You know, she owes him one from his number with the student all those years ago. People don't forget. Well, blokes don't anyway.'

'And so she tops him?' replied the DI disingenuously.

'Not necessarily *her*,' added Jackson gamely. 'What if she's got a bloke, and they want him out of the way?'

Kavanagh was satisfied that Judith Lacey's grief and mourning were entirely genuine. But a murder inquiry was a team game, and he knew that he had to carry his team with him for days, possibly weeks.

'Yes, all right, Jacko. I think she's on the level, but we're checking her out. Good point. Anyone else?'

There were no more questions.

'OK, Kev, carry on.' Kavanagh took Presley's seat as the sergeant came to the front of the room and tried to inject some life into the proceedings.

'Right, this is where we stand at the moment. We've done all the usual: house to house; checked anything or anyone suspicious during the last couple of weeks; done a detailed search of the surrounding area: verges, drains, gardens. Checked all the council bins, skips and bags. Drained the nearby cuts and waded the streams in the vicinity. Plenty of supermarket trolleys, more bikes than Halfords, even a bloody safe, but still no murder weapon. We know it was a knife, about five inches long, and very sharp. It was plunged in with great force, only the hilt stopped it; there's bruising around the soft tissue surrounding the stab wounds.

'We all know how important finding it is. We're going

to widen the search area. Dave's got the details and the running order. We *must* find it. Also, *somebody* must've seen him leaving the scene, probably running away. He was covered in blood, for Chrissakes!

'There weren't many people around that night. It was cold, and anyway, most people were in watching England not qualify for the World Cup.' There was some token jeering as the officers recalled the refereeing in Holland that had cost England a place in America, and Graham 'Do-I-not-like-that' Taylor his job.

'Yes, it was a bad night all round,' said the sergeant ruefully.

Presley picked up the threads of his summary: 'A woman who lives in the terraced cottages a couple of hundred yards down from the centre reckons there was a car that she hadn't seen before. It's all old folk in those houses, and they don't get many cars coming and going, but she's in her seventies and doesn't drive.

'She thinks it was a big, "square" car. We've shown her photos and taken her to the showrooms but, frankly, she hasn't got much of a clue. She said it could be a Volvo or one of the big Fords, then on the way back to the station she pointed at a bloody Maestro. She *does* know it was blue, though.

'Unfortunately, it was dry that night and the SOCO and forensic people haven't come up with anything distinctive in the way of tapings, scrapings, dustings or prints. At least, not yet. There are hundreds of smudged fingerprints on the door and jamb of the centre, and lots more on the back of the college van, but it's virtually impossible to eliminate from those, and anyway, is this maniac going to have any form, even if we could?'

Presley continued in similar vein for another five minutes, but there was nothing new. It was a pep talk. When investigations were hot, there was no time for this kind of thing. Most of them were experienced detectives, and they knew that the witnesses who didn't come for-

30

ward straightaway usually didn't come forward at all.

Murder weapons were usually found quickly, or they weren't found at all. Killers always panicked. Unless they didn't. And if they didn't, they weren't the kind of killers who threw the knife over the first hedge they passed. They knew what they were doing, and if they knew what they were doing, it made them very hard to catch. The atmosphere in the room was dispiriting.

'Are we sure it's a him?' asked Rees from the back of the room.

'From the force of the wound, which is just about all we've got to go on, Khaliq and his people down at pathology think so. But it could be a strong woman, or a tough kid. We can't rule anything out. We checked out the pianist, the woman who found him. No blood on her clothes, apart from a bit on her hem where she'd leaned over him. No motive, no strength. She's well out of the frame.'

The sergeant continued for a few minutes longer and then glanced over at Kavanagh, who gave him a nod of assent. 'We're going to keep up this level of operation for a few more days. Reinterview all those we've already spoken to and widen it out to anyone with past involvement with Lacey: ex-students, ex-members of staff, and of course we're still trying to trace the boyfriend of the girl he had an affair with.

'We haven't really got elimination criteria, 'cause we haven't got a motive. Everyone's in the frame. But it'll whittle down. It just needs some good, patient cop work.'

He paused, seemed to be prevaricating. There was a sense of expectation in the room, the atmosphere had changed. Presley finally said, 'Look, if we don't get anywhere by early next week, they've got a vacant slot on *Crimewatch* . . .'

Before he could finish his sentence there was a rowdy chorus of groans and hisses from the assembled officers.

Kavanagh joined his besieged sergeant at the front of the noisy crowd and took over. 'I know, I know. Listen;

31

they've got six or seven minutes, just come vacant. Armed robbery in Exeter. They'd filmed a reconstruction, lined the whole thing up, got some Devon yokel DS to learn his lines and everything, and then the villain gets grassed up by some lowlifer who owes him one.

'So they've got a space that's up for grabs and the Yard have been on to us to see if we want it. I asked them to give me a week; they've given us three days, and then they'll have to film and everything. Even that's cutting it fine.'

The barely good-humoured barracking continued. Kavanagh weighed in again, this time louder, and entirely seriously. 'You tell me. If we can't get anything locally, all we know is that we're looking for someone who was out at that time, who almost certainly had bloodstained clothes to clean or dispose of, and who *should* have a motive for killing Lacey.'

Finally, curtailing the meeting at the same time as showing his own exasperation, he said quietly and calmly, 'Find the knife, that's all we've got to do; just find the knife then we can keep off the telly and solve our own murders.'

The detectives began to meander away. 'Bloody TV,' said Mick Nugent to Rees as they sauntered out of the room. 'We'll be on Noel Edmonds and have the fuckin' villains on *Blind Date* next.'

Half of them were already on the stairs when Kavanagh called out, 'And remember the car. Keep it in mind, whoever you're talking to. She *says* it was blue. Cheers.'

6

There were three short tributes from the pulpit before the priest's address to the congregation.

Lacey's brother, two years younger than the dead man, said a few halting words about his sibling, 'my best mate, as well as my brother,' and lamented what he might have achieved, given a few more years.

There was no hint of forgiveness or understanding in his emotion-choked words, just resentment and bitterness at his brother's untimely, violent death.

This was the trouble with atheists, thought the young vicar, sitting a few feet away, his eyes closed, his fingers loosely intertwined; they always filled his church to mourn the things not done, paid scant heed to the many riches bestowed upon each life.

A pretty student, in black skirt, tights, and Doctor Marten shoes, stepped up to the lectern and delivered an eloquent tribute to her teacher, a man who had been, as well as an inspirational teacher, 'a really good friend' to she and her fellow pupils.

The college principal spoke next.

McEwan heaped fulsome praise upon his departed art teacher, said that his colleagues from the college would all be here, were they not 'doing what John would have wished them to be doing: teaching students, the students whose lives he has so enriched. For life must go on, even in the midst of tragedy.

'A final word,' he said solemnly. 'As a mark of respect

to John, and his contribution to the college during the last eighteen years, I have to tell you that the chairman of the governors of the college has accepted my proposal that the new sports hall, under construction now, and due for completion in May shall, hereafter, be known as the John Lacey Sports Hall.'

Was it the tone of plangent scene-setting, the archly self-important 'my proposal', or simply his grandiose use of 'hereafter', with its connotations of eternity, which made Kavanagh feel so distinctly uncomfortable in the crowded church?

When he and Presley had visited the college, they had seen the new sports hall rising from the turves of what had been the playing field. It was a big, white, aircraft hangar of a building, with ubiquitous red bricks being herring-bone filleted into the forecourt. Kavanagh doubted that it would be here in thirty years' time, much less in the 'hereafter'.

At the cemetery, on the cold, October afternoon, there were family and college students and neighbours and well-wishers and even a few people attracted merely by the size of the crowd and the numbers of cars that had followed the cortège.

Kavanagh looked at the pretty college girls and wondered, mystified as ever by changes in fashion, was there someone who sat in a room somewhere and said, 'Now!' and suddenly the world wore Caterpillar boots?

He stood with Presley at the back of the mourners and looked for signs of . . . of what? In a movie, a former lover would drop a single flower into the open grave, or some forgotten child would scowl at the widow. At the very least a long, dark car would crawl up behind the cortège, the window would slide down and a face in the rear seat would peer towards the mourners.

Kavanagh examined the cemetery road: a Mercedes hearse; a black Austin Princess, the chief mourners' car, on a 'B' plate, ten years old and looking as if it had come out of the showroom yesterday. Probably never been in fifth, thought the inspector.

Even the weather lacked drama appropriate to the graveside scene. In films, it rained cold sleet or, for ironic effect, it might be life affirming and sunny. Here, in a north Birmingham suburb, it was just very English: cold, bright, sunless sky; pale, high, thin cloud. It was weather to make a man mad. And Kavanagh felt it.

Lacey's widow looked well: deeply, mournfully attractive. Since Rachael had left him, marriage, any marriage, could make him grieve. A couple choosing pasta or apples in the supermarket hurt him. Middle-aged parents holding hands or, worse, walking with a grandchild, was torture to his soul. Joy was sorrow; sunshine, pain.

When he drew back the bedroom curtains in the morning, he gave silent thanks if it was raining or overcast and cold.

He turned off the weather forecast if the presenter was young and amiable. He watched it through (never listening) only if it was the dour man who had failed to predict the big storm of 1987, and who appeared to have been properly resentful ever since.

She was in black, of course. It became her well. She looked even lovelier than when he had spoken to her at her home three or four days ago. She hadn't eaten for nearly a week, not eaten properly, at least. Emotional trauma was the most effective crash diet that he knew. For years he had dallied with the half-a-stone extra that he carried: semi-skimmed milk; rubbery, no-fat cheese; low-fat spreads; even white wine in the pub for a couple of weeks, but it was not until he and Rachael parted that he dropped the half-stone, and nearly another half as well, within a fortnight.

He smoked all day and half the night; drank coffee, black, a few grains of sugar, and became a flat-tummied 42-year-old in days. His routine life – dull habit, soaked through with the reassurance of custom – had gone out of the window in that moment.

Driving home, he would tell himself that if the traffic lights didn't change before he got to them, or if the cyclist in front turned left, or if the next car that he passed was a Vauxhall, or red, or driven by a woman . . . she would have written to him; she would be there when he got home.

It was about the level of not walking on the pavement cracks when he was a kid. It didn't work now either. In fact, it was a dangerous game to play, because when he had hurriedly parked the car, and checked amongst the junk mail for her spidery handwriting, and walked down the hall and could see the phone's non-blinking, no-message, red light on the machine, that was when he came closest to taking not just the half-bottle of Bell's, but the bottle of paracetamol too.

He had started to look longingly, yearningly, at the most unsuitable women. Funerals so flattered women. Grief became them. Judith Lacey was lovely in her simple, dark mourning.

Funerals, anyway, were so much easier than weddings, with their ceaseless good humour, bonhomie, and brittle, enforced intimacy between people who frequently never met again.

As a young uniformed cop, Kavanagh had attended a couple of the big, family weddings that were always held in some soulless housing-estate pub and generally degenerated into a drunken brawl by ten o'clock in the evening.

They were ugly, nasty things with the groom's red-necked family battering the bride's big-knuckled cousins or friends or brothers, but there was, at least, some feeling about them.

They weren't the weak tea, poncey linen suits, champagne and tiramisu affairs that he and Rachael attended, travelling down to rural Berkshire (her side), or across to Staffordshire (his side), where everything was so well mannered that his mouth ached for a whole day after, not from a big drunken fist in it, but from too much phoney smiling.

Compared with this, funerals were a blessing, occasions clearly focused on grief and immutable mortality: what flimsy cause for celebration was the temporary union of *any* couple compared with the rock-solid certainty of a corpse in a box beside the assembled mourners?

The sextons (were they still called that, Kavanagh wondered?) were lowering the oak coffin, the vicar saying the few last words as the straps let the wooden box unevenly down.

Green plastic matting concealed the ragged edge of the freshly dug grave. It was incongruous, like plastic flowers in a restaurant, and reminded the inspector of the pineapples and avocados on greengrocer's pavement displays.

She came to the side of the hole and stood a moment before the horrible reality of the box in this dark place: inside it, her husband's body. Him. The mole on his back, the curling hair around his ears, his changeable brown eyes.

Her tears, at first no more than shallow gasps, became deep, uncontrollable sobs.

They were waiting for her to do the next thing. When she had done it, they would lead her to the car and shovel the mound of earth that lay a few yards away, covered by a tarpaulin, onto his coffin.

She dropped a handful of the soil onto the box and the grains scattered along the dark, highly polished lid. Her son put his arm around her shoulders, and they backed away from the edge. Lacey's parents and brother came to the edge of the grave and sprinkled in their handfuls of earth.

Two officers, a man and a woman, took the names of everyone who was not already known to the police as

37

they made their way down the little slope to the waiting cars.

Kavanagh joined the widow beside the funeral car. He was lost for words, but eventually said, 'It was a nice gesture . . .'

She looked at him bemused, as if he had spoken to her in Arabic.

'The sports hall,' he said. 'A nice gesture . . . The John Lacey Sports Hall . . .'

She turned towards the waiting car, and then looked at Kavanagh through the net of her black veil. The exhaust smoke from the Austin Princess plumed onto the damp tarmac and rolled away. 'He couldn't stand Aidan McEwan. And he loathed sport.'

7

'And now to a truly baffling crime . . .'

Kavanagh was struck by the archaic language; there was a cosy reassurance about it which belied the fearful reality of most crime.

'Baffling' had a Holmesian ring to it: Sherlock, not the Home Office Large Major Enquiry System computer, a typically arcane Whitehall acronym.

This was the media at work. The show became the issue; 'the medium the message,' in the words of another age. It changed everything it touched. It dressed it, and then consumed it. Nothing was as it seemed, and the irony was that everyone knew that this was so.

Nick Ross looked directly at the camera and assumed his customary amalgam of boyish enthusiasm and earnest concern. 'In fact, police officers in Wellington, Shropshire, are not even certain that a crime *was* committed. But they have decided to appeal to *Crimewatch* viewers to see if any of them is aware of anything which might confirm their uneasiness about the deaths of Terry Sugar and his wife, Jeanette.'

Ninety-degree turn; look to camera two; head and shoulders. 'Terry Sugar was a well-known character on the streets of Wellington. He had been a street trader there for years, and was often to be seen on the High Street selling his wares. In the summer it might be lighters, miracle cleaners or sports socks; in the winter, Sellotape, ironing-board covers, boxes of chocolates or perfume.

'Just over five weeks ago, on the morning of Thursday, September 16th, the bodies of Mr Sugar and his wife were found in the front seats of their car in their fume-filled garage. They had died from carbon monoxide poisoning.

'In itself, this kind of death is not particularly unusual these days. Exhaust fumes are lethal in an enclosed space and, as everyone knows, you should never start your car in a garage without first opening the doors.

'But in this case there were certain details which suggested to the police that this tragedy might not be an accident, and initial inquiries led them to believe that they were dealing with a double suicide.

'However, in a suicide there are usually things that one expects to find, and several of these things were not there. In most suicides, there is a clear reason for the deceased's action: illness, financial worries, unemployment, or an inability to cope because of some personal problem.

'With double suicides, which are statistically much rarer, the reasons are generally even more clear.

'In the case of Mr and Mrs Sugar, investigating officers have been unable to find *any* reason why they would have killed themselves.'

There was no filmed reconstruction, for there was little to reconstruct: the short walk from the couple's flat in Newport Road to their garage fifty yards away would not, the producer had reasoned, make riveting television.

Kavanagh sat in the hospitality suite and watched the studio monitor as Ross questioned West Mercia's Inspector Tom Bromage about the supposed suicide. He winced at his colleague's stilted delivery, the stultifying jargon that policemen seemed programmed to slip into whenever there was the sniff of a television crew or a newspaper reporter. No one 'walked' down the road; they 'proceeded'. People weren't 'stopped'; they were 'apprehended'. People didn't drive cars, but vehicles, which never had tax discs on their windscreens, but excise licences.

It was a textbook pedantry that killed. The raw energy of

40

any police station canteen would have served their cause better.

Kavanagh pulled at his shirt collar and loosened the knot of his tie. Bromage wasn't going to win any Oscars for his performance, but when the inspector tried to remember the replies that *he* was supposed to improvise around his script they, also, suddenly became unaccountably difficult to say: completely ordinary words sounded absurd as he tried them out in his dry mouth and heard them reverberate in his head.

Kavanagh had heard of the double 'suicide' case on the inter-force grapevine, and he already knew quite a bit more about it than the nine million Thursday-evening *Crimewatch* voyeurs were being told.

Sugar was a bit of a jack the lad. As well as selling ironing-board covers and cheap lighters and fake Swiss chocolates, he was a registered smack addict.

It was almost quaint, in these harsh, violent and unpredictable times, to find people like Terry Sugar. He used regularly, his emaciated body and the prominent blue veins in his wiry arms demanded it, but he also functioned, got onto the street and sold his goods and came home and fixed himself into a temporary oblivion. But he didn't die or kill you. He didn't even steal your money.

Tom Bromage knew Sugar hadn't fallen foul of dope dealers. His personal stash was still in the house, his bit of cash hadn't been nicked, and the Amstrad video was still on the shelf beneath the telly. It was all a bit of a mystery.

Kavanagh dabbed at his prickly palms with his handkerchief. His mind was racing. This is what they meant about the media. It was a serpent that devoured the issues it dealt with whole. He wasn't even thinking about art teacher John Lacey and his violent death. He was thinking only about not making a fool of himself, and of the boys, his colleagues and subordinates, gathered around the TV in the social club back at the division.

41

He played a cheap trick: forced himself to think of Lacey's distraught wife in an attempt to regain focus. It didn't work. Not making a fool of himself. That was all that mattered. An hour ago, the producer's assistant had run through the dummy questions: 'Just be yourself,' she had urged. 'You'll be fine. Be sincere, but be yourself. You need the viewers' help, and it's what *you* say that they'll be responding to.'

'"Be yourself!"' Kavanagh had no idea who he was. The alien environment: the studio lights; the gliding camera dollies; the background noise; the director on the headsets; the quietly frantic arms cuing people in; the make-up girl; the microphone men; his ex-wife out there in the night somewhere; *that* was all he knew.

And now began a new level of freneticism: the animal that had been incubated in the stifling heat threatened to get out of control and escape the straitjacket of its format as information started to pour in on the banks of telephones ranged around them.

Was she watching? Would she watch? It was all he could ever do to get her in front of a movie on TV before the opening credits rolled. They'd played the Woody Allen/Diane Keaton scene from *Annie Hall* a hundred times: he wouldn't watch the movie if they'd missed a second of it; she took spunky Keaton's 'Who gives a damn, we've seen it a dozen times anyway?' role.

He was sweating freely now. He patted his brow with his handkerchief and tried to clear his salivaless throat. He only had a few minutes. Had anyone ever declined? At the last minute, just said, 'No, I can't do it,' he wondered?

His hands would not dry. Somehow he had to rebutton his collar and tighten his tie without marking his white shirt.

And then he was being escorted to the place beside the presenter. Not listening, not seeing or hearing properly, just walking, with the production assistant at his side.

Would she watch? He'd left a message on her machine.

He'd counted the rings. Four was good. Four, and then hiss, crackle. And then her message. He was the only person he knew who actually preferred the machine: it was contact, but safe, one-way contact.

There was her voice. Everything just her. The slight, self-conscious hesitation, as if surprised at having had to record her message. And then the polite, effortlessly cultured voice with its slight bruising of the vowels and blunting of the 'h's' in her customary attempt to conceal her background.

But it was the sound of her voice. Faltering, vulnerable, kindly. It was a voice that gave to charity, saw the other point of view, remembered family birthdays, never saved Christmas wrapping paper from one year to the next.

She was the kind of person who, if she won a supermarket dash, would leave some of the expensive items, just to be fair.

And it was the voice that had said, with trembling, colourless lips, as he lay on the sofa watching the second episode of *Mr Wroe's Virgins*, 'I want to talk.'

He had heard something new; in a voice that he knew better than the sound of his own. He had heard the difference, turned round and switched off the television, swung his legs down and lit a cigarette and looked at her. It was seamless and dreamlike. Yet concrete and immediate and very brittle.

It wasn't the voice of someone who has crashed the car or flooded the bath or lost their job. He'd never heard it before, but he knew immediately what it meant, as if some atavistic gene was lying dormant, just waiting to be stirred by these very words.

And from then on his life had changed. And he heard that commonplace phrase again and again and again, and it always said, 'I want to talk,' and then, before he had had time to respond, 'I think we should part.'

And every time he heard it now, driving to work, looking at Lacey's blood on the churchyard pavement, turning

43

at night in his bed, or as the music played over the titles to *Match of the Day*, he wanted to stop it. Stop the music and stop the action, and let that time not happen.

Early days, Presley had said to him over a drink in the Chinese, late gambling club that they sometimes used, when everything else was quiet in the city, 'I'm sorry about you and Rachael, Frank. It's like a death in the family.'

Elvis was ex-army; a big, tough guy, who'd shot at people and may have hit some of them. He and Frank were Odd Couple cops, Presley's slob Matthau to Kavanagh's constipated Jack Lemmon, but somehow, past the level of Presley's greasy chip bags in the car and cigarette ash on his trousers, they were mates, good mates, and Frank had been touched by the feeling that the ex-paratrooper had conveyed in the crass cliché.

They'd sat in the corner as the waiters from the city-centre restaurants squandered their wages and tips at the roulette wheel. Elvis became lugubrious, more maudlin than Frank, but when he said again, 'It's like a death in the family,' Frank, hunched over the low table, replied bitterly, 'It's worse, Kev. She's there, but she doesn't come back. She could, but she doesn't.'

And there was her voice on the machine, saying she was out and leave a message and she'd call back. And he listened to it as if she might be saying something to *him.*

Yes, the machine was better. She couldn't reach him, couldn't probe him, in her gentle way, which reminded him of her, and what had been his love for her, and now hurt so much that he didn't know what it was: love or jealousy or grief or just plain habit.

When they talked 'properly', without the machine between them, it was worse than this. A few times, they had hit a nerve, and there had been tears. Not anger, but sadness; comforting tears of loss. And he had felt better for hours, sometimes a day.

But it was all too tricky, far too precarious, and the

machine was better. That little contact was enough.

He wondered whether they might maintain their new relationship for ever, just through the optical fibres of the telephone system. (Or were they fibre optics?)

He eventually said, after her hesitant message, 'Hello, Rachael.' (Even saying her name was odd, strangely formal. He had rarely called her Rachael, she him Frank.) 'I'm on *Crimewatch* this evening. It starts at 9.30. I thought you might like to know . . .' He tried to sound cavalier. 'Goodbye. I'll give you a ring.'

He should hang up. He'd got away with it. She might come in, pick up the phone, talk back. She might have her key in the door now. She could be walking towards the phone, or have her hand on it.

'How's things?' he said, and then, unable to let go, 'Are you OK?'

In fact, when he heard the sirens heading for the dangerous dual carriageway these days, he always said a little prayer. And the prayer was: 'Let it be her. Let her die, and free me from this pain of wanting her.'

Nick Ross was bringing the Wellington 'suicide' to a close. 'Do *you* know anything about the movements of the Sugars that Wednesday night? Did *you* see them make the short walk to the garage near the back of their flat? Were they alone? Did you see *anything* or *anyone* at all suspicious in the area at around about that time?

'If so, do please give us a call. The number to ring is 071 497 3333, or, if you prefer, Wellington, that's 0952 3322. The lines are open until eleven o'clock this evening. And please, remember, the police know that Terry Sugar's dealings weren't all strictly legitimate. But they're not interested in that. They are interested only in the death of him and his wife. Any information you give will be treated in the strictest confidence.'

Ross's assurances of confidentiality were subjected to appropriate derision in the Birmingham police social club

45

where Kavanagh's colleagues awaited their boss's appearance before the nation's TV audience.

Ross handed proceedings over to Sue Cook. Kavanagh slipped into the seat beside her, out of vision, while she introduced Charles Maine from the *Antiques Roadshow* who went through his 'Aladdin's Cave' of recovered stolen property.

When the moment arrived, and the director counted Cook in on her earpiece, she turned to Kavanagh, outlined the stabbing of Lacey that was 'mystifying' the West Midlands force, and the filmed reconstruction began.

When it was over, Cook asked the inspector the couple of questions they had agreed on. He faltered a little, conscious as he was of hearing his own voice, but as his mind addressed the questions, rather than tried to recall the script, he picked up, found his genuine interest in the case, and got through.

His brief ordeal over, she thanked him, and appealed again for help from the public. The inspector was smiling benignly and, before he knew it, Ross was introducing the next item.

Back in hospitality, exhausted by the release of the pent-up tension and surprised at how quickly the seven or eight minutes had passed, Kavanagh and DI Tom Bromage compared notes on their performances.

Vanity satisfied, they eventually discussed the respective cases.

Bromage filled Kavanagh in on the details of the double 'suicide'. What they hadn't revealed on air was that when he was found, Terry Sugar had been sitting in the driving seat.

'So what?' asked Kavanagh.

'He didn't drive,' replied Bromage. 'It's not conclusive, of course, but it's a bit odd.

'Also, there was no note. Everybody leaves a note.' He swilled his Scotch and dry around the tumbler before gulping it down. 'Almost everybody. Especially on a double.'

'Yes, I suppose so,' said Kavanagh.

Bromage poured himself another Scotch and wagged the bottle at Kavanagh.

'Why not?' said the inspector. He always paid his TV licence fee. 'Why not?' They had been through their trial by television and now, in the warm glow of BBC hospitality, free whisky, huge sofas and deep-pile carpets, there was no torment.

'The third point, you'll like this,' said Bromage conspiratorially. 'They left the video set. Now that *would* be a first. Setting the video to record a programme and topping yourself *before* you watch it. Come on! You might top yourself *after* you've watched some of the crap that's on these days, but not before!'

Frank had grown up with the *Wednesday Play*, when it was commonplace for everyone to be talking about it on the way to work or even at school the next day. He remained unfashionably defensive about the once-hallowed institution, and thought the first ad to appear on the BBC would probably be the beginning of the end for the venerable corporation. He eschewed the opportunity to share his view with his Wellington colleague.

'What was it?' asked Kavanagh, intrigued.

'What was what?' replied Bromage.

'That he had recorded? What had they set the video for?'

'Some *Late Show* thing on a jazz bloke. Sugar was a jazz freak. The geezer was called Rollins. Sonny Rollins, a trumpeter, a profile of him.'

Kavanagh had a couple of the saxophonist's records tucked in amongst his John Coltrane, Theolonius Monk, Charlie Mingus and Miles Davis LPs. 'So you reckon they were topped. But why? No theft? No drugs involvement that you can find?'

There was a screeching of tyres as the last reconstruction played on the hospitality-suite monitors. 'Why do blaggers always leave the scene of the crime at eighty miles an hour and drive on the pavement? Don't they realize that if they drove at thirty and stopped for children on pedestrian crossings, they'd attract no more attention than anyone else going to work or down to the shops?'

Frank smiled at Bromage's facetious observation. 'So, what about the Sugars then?'

Bromage moved a few inches closer to Kavanagh on the six-seater leather sofa. 'We're sure they were killed. At least we're dead sure it's not suicide.' He leaned forward as he spoke, put his whisky tumbler on the carpet. 'If you're a junkie and you're going to top yourself, what's the last thing you do?'

The question was rhetorical. He pushed his dark blue jacket sleeve up his arm. 'You give yourself a nice, good-bye fix. The one thing they don't advertise about smack and coke, the one thing they never mention, is that people use them 'cause they make you feel good. For a while.' He sniggered. 'If you're going to kill yourself, why not feel *very* good and inject yourself a big one? Sugar had got plenty in his drawer. But he hadn't had a hit for ages.'

Kavanagh played the devil's advocate. Also, it seemed a reasonable question: 'So why would they get into a car to get killed? They've nothing to lose if they refuse.'

Bromage grew serious. 'Do you remember Amin in the seventies?'

'Of course.'

'I've always remembered reading something really horrible. Not just heads in the fridge and firing squads and bodies in the river. They used to line up poor bastards, and the second poor fucker in line would smash the head of the guy in front of him, and then the third would smash the second, all the way back down the line.'

'Yes,' said Kavanagh, 'horrible. But so what?'

'Why did they do it? You *know* you're next.'

'Why?' asked Kavanagh.

''Cause the guy looking down on you has the gun or

the machete, and if you don't do what he says, you die, not later, but that instant.

'Another minute's life. That's what we're told. Jews hiding in the latrines in the camps, up to their necks in shit. Hanging on. Another minute, another few seconds. *Maybe* the cavalry'll come. They do in the movies. *Maybe* the Russians will break through and open the barbed-wire gates. They will do, one day. It's no good if you've given up the day before. *Maybe* the guy with the gun or machete will have a heart attack, get shot, find religion, see the light, let you off, go home.'

Kavanagh resented the allusion to the Holocaust, even to make a serious point, but his three years at a Catholic primary school had left him with not only the terror of purgatory and eternal hell, but also the notion of sweet redemption: '"Between the stirrup and the ground, he mercy sought, and mercy found,"' said Sister Agnes.

'And that's why these two are prepared to get in a car and get themselves slowly killed?' said Kavanagh, sceptical.

'It's *possible*. That's all I'm saying. It's not suicide, that's for sure.' Bromage picked up his glass and peered into the filmy ginger ale as it swirled with the whisky. 'They were topped. It was original, and it was hands off. But it *was* murder.'

He had kept his ace till last, intending to cast it down with a flourish. But Kavanagh was thoughtful, didn't challenge him.

'You got any cats, Frank?'

Bromage was two or three whiskies ahead of Kavanagh, his boozy familiarity signalled in his use of the other man's forename.

Kavanagh didn't care for cats and their hauteur. He preferred animals with a little dependency. 'No, I don't have a cat,' he said, wondering where the arcane question was leading.

'You know all those wankers with stickers in their cars

– A dog is for life, not just for Christmas; Meat is Murder – all that crap. Who do they think is listening?'

Bromage was more drunk than Kavanagh had realized. What was all this about car stickers?

'Do they think a sticker in the back window of a car is going to have any effect on the kind of bloke who breeds dogs for killing, or chucks them out on the motorway?

'Best one I ever saw said: *Rowing, a growing sport.* Now what the fuck's that supposed to mean! *Rowing, a growing sport.* What fucking genius dreamed that up? Does the wanker driving that around on the back of his Maestro think I'm going to read it and go out and buy a boat and start rowing? I mean, if he likes fucking rowing, that's all right, but why's he want *me* to do it?'

Kavanagh didn't fancy the idea of the press (or anyone else) getting hold of the fact that one of the country's top detectives was half-pissed in the *Crimewatch* studios and tried to get back to the point. 'What *about* the cat, Tom?'

'They hadn't fed it, mate. They'd only been in the garage overnight, but when we broke into the house the next morning, the cat was starving. Suicides always feed their animals. Always.' Ross was on his feet doing his close-down piece to camera, reassuring a formerly anxious, now terrified viewing public, who had spent the last three quarters of an hour being vicariously subjected to all sorts of horror and depravity that, in fact, the incidence of violent crime was really very low.

He had once, famously, short of time, decided to drop this little homily from the end of the show. There followed over a thousand calls to the duty officer asking why Ross had not said it, as if, in not hearing it, the public would immediately become even more vulnerable. There might be armed robbers crashing through the studio walls, or anarchists setting the aged commissionaire ablaze, but it was clear that Ross would, for evermore, be expected to deliver his comforting words.

Other officers started to drift in, then the production

people, and eventually the director with her stars, Cook and Ross. The show had gone well. The atmosphere was congenial.

Bromage and Kavanagh took their coffee and returned to the studio where the incoming calls were being sifted and recorded. The lines would remain open for another twenty-four hours, but at 11.15 that night, there would be an 'update' for viewers.

There were the usual number of cranks dialling in who wanted to confess to everything. Many of them sounded plausible, and probably led otherwise blameless lives as bus drivers and accountants and media analysts, but their credibility as murderers or robbers was seriously undermined when they were unable to say exactly what weapon had been used, or what colour dress the hapless victim was wearing on the night of her death.

There were some good leads on a rape case and hard information on an armed robbery in Dorking. But there were only scraps on the Lacey killing: a couple of calls from people who had known the teacher in the past, and who were making themselves known so that they could help if needed. It was an ego thing. The punters liked to be involved, they couldn't wait to make a phone call to *Crimewatch* and tell their neighbours about it the next day. But they were a waste of time. They had nothing to add. The people who had the info generally kept mum. They didn't phone crime shows.

There was one call from someone who had driven down the road on the night in question, and who had noticed someone walking towards the cars parked near the terraced cottages down from the church lych gate.

A senior officer took the caller's number and arranged to visit him in Kidderminster the following day. It wasn't much, but it was something. Under careful questioning, he might remember some details that he didn't even know he had logged.

Kavanagh's initial reaction as he listened in to the

recording of the caller was that he didn't like the fact that the 'suspect' had been walking. It meant one of two things. If you were walking, you either weren't guilty, or you were smart.

If Kavanagh had little, Bromage had less. A few confessor cranks, a couple of people who said they'd scored for Sugar, or from him, none of whom was prepared to give an address or a name.

One caller suggested that someone called Nicky Dolan owed Sugar one, and that the police should check him out. He declined to give his name and slammed down the phone before the trace could be effected. It was probably malice, drop some poor fucker in the shit and waste twenty hours of police time, but they'd check it out.

One loony phoned in to say that someone was parked in *his* place on the night in question. 'A fucking double murder inquiry and the guy's calling about someone parked across his drive,' said Bromage to Kavanagh as they walked down to their cars at midnight. 'He can't get his fucking Skoda in 'cause some tosser's parked his Volvo there.'

Kavanagh had had enough of Tom Bromage; he wanted to get his head down. It was only early autumn, but the night was clear and the wind blew cold around the car park. The BBC building was lit up like a big ship in the night bearing down on the traffic in Wood Lane below it.

The two men shook hands. 'What colour was it?' said Kavanagh.

'What colour was what?' said Bromage.

'The car,' said Kavanagh.

'The Skoda?' guffawed Bromage.

'No,' said Kavanagh, seriously. 'The Volvo.'

Bromage leaned against his car, laughing.

Kavanagh smiled, pulled up his collar and shivered inside his blue cashmere overcoat.

Bromage clambered into the front seat beside his driver.

Kavanagh held the door open and repeated quietly, 'What colour was it, Tom?'

Bromage had stopped laughing. He had his hand on the door pull, but Kavanagh's hand resisted the pressure. Bromage wanted to go. He was tired and half pissed. '*I* don't know, Frank. I didn't ask. Why?'

'It's nothing,' said Kavanagh. He released the door, and said brightly, trying to suggest that the antagonism had been a figment of the drunk's imagination, 'Can I give you a call tomorrow? Check it out for me, will you?'

'Sure,' said Bromage without enthusiasm, and slumped back into the seat as his driver pulled away.

Kavanagh joined his driver and left the Shepherd's Bush studio for the journey home to Birmingham. On the way up the M1 he laid his head on his folded coat in the back seat of the big Ford and watched the green dashboard display until he eventually dropped off to sleep.

Once, instead of phoning or using the post, she had dropped a note through his door in the evening. He had got up to make a drink and seen the envelope lying there. It had driven him mad. She had been that close, and he hadn't known.

Since then, whenever he passed the hall, he always looked down at the mat beneath the letter box. He tried not to do it, but he couldn't stop himself. It had become a fetish.

Back at the house in Erdington, the mat was bare. He checked out the red, unblinking eye of the answering machine, poured himself a treble Bell's, and dialled Presley.

'Hello,' said the sleeping man. 'Who is it?'

'Did you ever see *Strangers on a Train*, Elvis?'

'Fucking hell, you've been on the telly for five minutes, Frank, and now you wanna be a film star! Do you know what time it is?'

'Yes. Have you ever seen it?'

'*Strangers on a Train*? Yes. I think so. The one with the two old duffers who always want to know the test match score?'

'No,' said Kavanagh, sighing. 'That's *The Lady Vanishes*. *Strangers on a Train* is Hitchcock, too. But it's from a Patricia Highsmith novel. 1951.'

'What is this? The National fucking Film Theatre show or something?'

Frank liked Elvis, he had a natural way with words, knew exactly when to punctuate a sentence with an expletive.

'Bear with it, El. *Strangers* is altogether different stuff. I'll show it you. I've got it on tape. You'll see what I mean.'

'You phoned me at half past two in the morning to ask me if I've seen *Strangers on a* bloody *Train*. And you're going to lend me the video. Thanks, Frank. Thanks a lot.'

'You will, mate. You will. 'Night, 'night. See you in the morning. Sleep tight!'

8

'Bollocks!'

Presley was acting gauche. He didn't have to work too hard at it, thought Kavanagh.

'Absolute bollocks! The one guy's a tennis player . . .'

'Farley Granger . . .' said Kavanagh.

'And wants to top his old man,' continued Presley. 'The other guy's a psychopath—'

'Robert Walker,' interrupted Kavanagh.

'OK, Robert Walker,' added Presley. 'He wants his missis out of the way.'

'You've cracked it, El. I knew you'd get there eventually.'

The sergeant ignored his boss's facetiousness. 'And so they do one another's murders?'

'Right,' said Kavanagh.

'So what?' said Presley.

'It's just the standard thing. Textbook procedure. We always have to look for a motive. If the suspect has a cast-iron, genuine alibi, they're out of the frame. That was the beauty of the thing. Each of the murderers was definitely somewhere else when "his" victim was killed.'

'So they got away with it?'

'Afraid not.'

'Why not?' asked Presley, genuinely interested.

'1951.'

'1951?'

'America. The Hays Code. Came in in the thirties. The

authorities were getting worried about the crime rate, and they reckoned that the movies weren't helping, so they drew up a code of ethics: no stocking tops, no cleavage, no two people of opposite sex on a bed together, and most important of all, Jimmy Cagney and his crew had to come unstuck. From now on in, the good guys had to win.'

'So Farley Granger and Co screw it up?'

'Yes. I can't remember exactly how it goes. Something to do with a fairground, and a little studio lake and a lighter on an island. But that's not the important bit for what I'm saying.'

'What you're saying's bollocks, Frank.'

'I'm not saying that someone did someone else's murder; that's fraught with danger anyway. Both people have to be pretty bright, and yet, paradoxically, unhinged enough to be prepared to kill someone, *and* in cold blood. It's still unusual to find one like that; it's off the scale that you'll find two.'

'Except in the movies,' added Presley slyly.

Kavanagh ignored him. 'At least, I reckon it is. No, what I'm saying is, we've got our Lacey killing here, with no motive, or no apparent motive. And then West Mercia get their exhaust fumes deaths, and there's no motive there.'

'Or no apparent motive,' said Presley.

'Fair enough. No apparent motives for either of them? What's the odds against that, Elvis? They're not random killings. They're executions. Thought out, planned, deliberate. There are none of the obvious suspects: family, girlfriend, boyfriend; nor any of the usual reasons: greed, money problems, insurance scams, inheritance, all that stuff. We've looked at the beneficiaries, there's been no recent topping up on policies, no one's got any treasure maps under the bed. The Sugar couple left less than a grand. The flat was rented.

'Who benefited from Lacey's death?' continued Kavanagh. 'His missis. The endowment pays off the mortgage. Big deal. You saw her at the cemetery. Are you telling me that was a woman who killed her husband so that they wouldn't have to pay the Halifax a couple of hundred a month? No, she's genuine. They had their ups and downs, but she has no more idea why her husband died than we do. So where does that leave us?'

'Tell me, Frank. Where does it leave us?'

Kavanagh ignored the heavy sarcasm. 'I think we've got related crimes, but we just can't see the link. That's what's throwing us.'

'One by gas, the other with a knife; forty miles apart, and you think there's a connection? Come on, Frank!'

'You do better, then,' said Kavanagh. 'I've been in the force twenty years, investigated over thirty murders. I've never had so little to go on. That's fair enough. A first. There's got to be one. But then, within a couple of weeks of it, it transpires there's been another murder, and not a motive or a suspect or a clue to be found. I'm telling you, El, it's too much.'

'So, all we've got is: no connection, no motive, equals a connection? Forget it, Frank. It won't stand up.'

'Do better,' challenged Kavanagh.

'You're off the wall, Frank,' said Presley.

'They were both on Wednesdays, similar times as far as we can tell, mid-evening.'

'There's a Wednesday every seven days. Two murders on a Wednesday don't make a pattern,' said Presley.

Kavanagh ignored the cavil and continued. 'There's the blue Volvo parked in the Skoda bloke's usual place near the Sugar murders in Wellington. And the old woman down the road from the Lacey stabbing picked out a Volvo 244 as being a contender for the car she saw parked outside her cottage on the night Lacey died.'

'She's seventy-eight years old, Frank. There *were* no cars when she was born.'

'Come on, Kev, there's no need to stick it on.'

'Seriously, have you seen the thickness of her glasses? You could skate on them. Can you imagine what a defence

57

would do with her on the witness stand? And anyway, she also picked out a Maestro and a Ford.'

'Well, at least she knows it was blue, whatever it was. Will you accept that?'

'Yes, I will, as long as you accept it doesn't mean a thing.'

'I want you to put one of the lads on Volvo import figures.'

'Going back how far?'

'As long as the 244's been on the market here.'

'Do you know how many Volvos that is, Frank?'

'No, of course I don't, but we're going to. Look on the bright side, El. It's only 244s we're interested in. The guy with the Skoda was a good witness . . .'

'Yes, I bet he was. I'd always trust the judgement of someone who buys a Skoda. So, what do you want me to do next?' asked Presley, acknowledging his superior's rank, even if unconvinced by his argument.

'We do all we can: start checking blue Volvos, then we'll find out where they are. Concurrently we log and cross-reference every single detail on the two murders. And then everything on the victims. Add anything unsolved and apparently motiveless that's come up recently. Find the link. It's there somewhere.

'We'll start with the last three months. Feed in everything: method of killing, geography, gender, age, wealth, what paper the victim read, what car they drove, everything, and we look for any connection between these apparently unconnected, motiveless murders. And when we find that connection, we'll find the motive, and then we'll nip out and pick up the killer.'

'They'll never wear it; the boys'll laugh you out.'

'They can laugh all they like. They either come up with something better, or they can start feeding in everything, and I mean *everything*: what Lacey had for breakfast; where he went on his holidays in 1983; why he watched

Coronation Street only on Mondays. Get it all in, and we'll find the link.'

'You're going for this, Frank? You really want this done?'

'Run the figures on homicide, Kev. Have a look at them for the last six months. Take out the fracas and affray and domestics; pull the drug-related and aggravated burglary; weed the sex-related ones and see what you're left with.'

'Take out all those, mate, and there *won't* be anything left.'

'That's my point. Have a look. It won't leave many.'

Presley had exhausted his arguments. He walked over to the far wall, pulled out his wallet, took a twenty-pound note and stapled it to the notice board. 'Pattern be bollocksed. Here's a score says you're up the wrong tree.'

Kavanagh joined him, and put two tens beside the mauve note. 'There's a connection, El. My "little man" says so.'

'Little man?' said Presley.

'Don't you ever watch proper films?' said Kavanagh. 'Edward G. Robinson; *Double Indemnity*. 1944. Husband apparently falls to his death. The insurance company has got to pay out, a "double indemnity". It all fits. But Edward G. just *knows* it isn't right. His "little man" nags away at him, won't let go, gets at him, right in the guts.'

'And?' said Presley.

'And eventually Fred McMurray and Barbara Stanwyck get nobbled,' said Kavanagh.

Presley was more a *Nine and a Half Weeks* and *Basic Instinct*, use-the-freeze-frame-button kind of man. 'The only little man you've got's between your legs, and you'd do better playing with him than having us count bloody Volvos.'

'Yes, you may be right, Kev,' said the inspector thoughtfully.

59

Presley was surprised by the conciliatory tone. Was reason going to prevail?

Kavanagh walked over to the open door. 'But look,' he said, and pointed to the sign on the door: *Detective Inspector Frank Kavanagh*. 'For the time being, if I want us to count cars, we count cars.'

9

'Just tell me, whenever we're looking for a suspect motor, why is it the most popular car on the road, in the most popular fucking colour?' said Ray Merson.

Detective Constable Michael Gilks was a literalist, a graduate psychologist from Reading University with a 2:2 Honours degree, but his three years at the Berkshire university had not included a module on rhetorical hyperbole, and he therefore failed to recognize it even when its use was clearly signalled.

'It's statistics, Ray,' Gilks began patiently. He'd once explained to his colleague the complex mathematical reason why you need only twenty-five people in a room for two of them to share the same birth date. Ray Merson, a graduate, not of university, but of Hendon Police College, had been impressed, and over supper that evening tried to explain the principle to his young wife. He quickly got bogged down and, as soon as she recognized this, she stopped listening and used the remote control to bring up the volume on *East Enders*.

Gilks continued, undaunted, as they drove up the M54 from Birmingham, 'If there are more Sierras on the road than anything else, the *probability* is that it'll be a Sierra we're looking for.' He paused, concentrated on the road ahead as he overtook a huge yellow and blue Hungarian truck and its trailer. The manoeuvre completed, Gilks said, 'Let's count ourselves lucky it's *not* a Sierra. It could be worse than this, believe me!'

Merson stole a glance at his colleague's face, but there was no suggestion of irony there.

Half an hour later they parked their unmarked car on the forecourt of the Esso station on the old A5 outside Shrewsbury, and the two young men went into the brightly lit garage that sold everything from fruit and vegetables to flowers and compact discs.

Merson showed his warrant card to the girl perched behind the high counter. 'Police, love, we phoned earlier. It's about the video recording.'

'Oh, yes, I've got it here.' She slipped off her stool, reached behind her, and passed the policeman the black plastic cartridge.

'Thanks. We'll let you have it back as soon as possible.'

They were visiting every large garage within a ten-mile radius of Wellington. Most of them had video-surveillance cameras running twenty-four hours a day, and Ray Merson and his partner had the unenviable task of collecting and then viewing these hours and hours of excruciatingly dull monochrome film in their boss's hunt for a blue Volvo 244, registration number unknown.

And all this because an old lady down the road from the parish centre where John Lacey had died thought that there had been a car parked outside her house that night that might have been a Volvo.

And, weeks after the deaths of Terry and Jeanette Sugar in Wellington, a Skoda owner had phoned *Crimewatch* to say he had left a note on the windscreen of a blue 244 asking its owner not to park in 'his' place.

Frank Kavanagh had been charmed by the notion that this quaint practice was still extant in rural counties: it was like using a carrier pigeon in an era when every roofer and truck driver had a mobile phone; or taking a rattle, amidst the racist and anti-Semitic terrace abuse, to a football match. You'd as likely get coshed or shot if you asked someone in an inner-Birmingham suburb not to park in 'your' place on a public road.

Presley was still awaiting the actual production figures from the Swedish motor giant, but you didn't have to be a car buff to know that the Two series had been on sale for ever.

Originally, ownership of the austere saloon by idiosyncratic bank managers had implied, if not exactly a penchant for naturist holidays, at least a predilection for narrow-boating on English canals, rather than the dubious charms of two weeks in Torremolinos.

Since those early days, ownership of the determinedly non-aerodynamic ton of Swedish steel had percolated down to teachers, civil servants and draughtsmen, and the car had lost a little of its Scandinavian mystique.

And indeed, for a good few years now, older models, vile, mustard paintwork rusting, but their tough Nordic chassis still intact, had found their way onto the less salubrious council estates of the country, where they changed hands for two or three hundred pounds, their new owners actually bragging about how many times around the clock the venerable beast had been.

Whatever the figure, Volvo 244s had been rolling across the cold North Sea in their thousands for nearly twenty years now. That was a lot of cars. But a couple of sightings of a blue car, possibly a Volvo, was all they had.

Needle in a haystack? Sheet of metal in a foundry? Merson and Gilks in a Shropshire garage. It was routine police work. And it was what it was all about.

Kavanagh was desperate for the inquiry to move. His motives were less than pure. It was over two weeks since Rachael had been in touch with him. His ego bruised, he wondered how she could cope without him. Not cope in the sense of go to her office and show houses to her clients and get the shopping, but really cope; be without him, completely, after all these years.

They had grown apart, lost touch with one another, but then, that fateful night, when she had said, 'I've got something to tell you. I think we should part,' he had been shaken; his being rocked to the core.

In truth, there had been a little irresistible euphoria that had accompanied the shock of her words. A danger, a raw freshness that he had not known for years. It was giddying and he, so often in control, had enjoyed the initial exhilarating sensation of free fall.

He had, after all, known that this separation was where their relationship was heading. Had known it for months and months now. But she had wrested the initiative, put the plan into action with her dozen words. My God, it was happening.

He was in shock: his reason told him that this is what he had known would happen. But now, it *was* happening. Only the tense had changed. The hypothesis, so frequently imagined, even courted, was now reality.

He felt like the man who had hung on to the rope, trying with the others on that grainy Zeppelin film, to keep the airship on the ground. Seeing the danger, they had let go, fallen a few feet to the earth. He had hung on, a sort of stubborn perversity precluding his letting go.

And now he was fifty, seventy, a hundred feet in the air and could no longer let go. It was terrifying.

His heart said: No, stop this. But his head said: Yes, this is it. This is how it feels. It's new and different, of course. But hang on. And with every moment that passed, the earth was further away and he knew he could no longer jump back.

He had lit a cigarette. Put the lighter down on the floor and heard himself saying to her, inanely, 'Five for a pound. How can they make lighters that sell for five for a pound?'

He took comfort within a week of her going. There was a systems analyst; she was a civilian, a divorcee. They'd given one another the once-over at a couple of things they'd worked on together. He had been still married; she had been 'free'. Her look and manner had said, 'Yes, if you like.' And he'd been wistful and thought, 'What if?' in the same way that he used secretly to read the contact ads in the press.

And then he *had* been free, and of course, it was very different. He knew he should take some time. See what was grief, and what was pain and what was shock and what was habit. And he did none of these things but rang her and asked her out to dinner.

He heard the hesitation in her voice. It wasn't like this before, when he was married, unhappy, or at least not happy, but safe. Then, there always seemed to be women working on inquiries, and he looked, and they looked, and it looked easy.

Between the actual words she was speaking, she was implying, 'What's up? What's happened? What's changed?'

He answered her with an affirmation he didn't feel; tried to suggest everything was OK.

They met in a city-centre pub and he drank too much. He had resolved not to get maudlin.

He told her, glossing the truth of Rachael's final, dramatic initiative in leaving, that they had agreed to part. Yes, he admitted, when it finally happened, it was a shock. (A certain amount of feeling, he judged, would appear appropriate to the situation. He didn't want to appear callous.)

He tried hard to imagine what a genuine mutually agreed parting would have been like, and adopt the appropriate demeanour. It was hard, like reading a prepared script at the same time as feeling something entirely different, the mental and verbal equivalent of performing the circular motion with your hand on your tummy while the other hand patted your head. He had never been able to do that either.

He drank more. The only thing that helped him was her appearance. In the worst scenario that he had conjured, he

wouldn't even fancy her any more, she would be metamorphosed into a plain and unattractive woman.

In fact, he found her alluring. Later, they went back to
her flat off Hagley Road, near Five Ways. She made coffee
and he slouched on the sofa and drunkenly hummed
along to Nina Simone. There was even a moment where
he believed that this *was* what it was all about: a meal,
drinks, a different environment, an attractive woman, a
new woman, one whose smell and body and touch he did
not yet know.

Later, in bed, her kisses were deep and hungry and were
accompanied by little murmurs of passion.

With every movement of their bodies her orgasm
appeared imminent, but after several minutes of this
nearly state, and recognizing his own imminent, urgent
need, she opened her eyelids, rolled her wild eyes head-
board-wise and said firmly, 'Wait.'

He obeyed. Was afraid not to. But the effort was great
and the tried and tested methods of delay were chilly
water to the natural heat of his sexual arousal.

Eventually, in spite of his mandatory detachment from
the proceedings, he found his natural rhythm again and
uttered a gruff imperative that left her in no doubt that
now was the moment.

As he finally gave in to his urgent needs, she embarked
upon some very loud and impressive groans which, he
felt confident, must have impressed her neighbours no
end.

But alas, although the folk on the other side of the wall
cannot have been anything but satisfied with the couple's
performance Liz, apparently, was not.

His quiet sighs of satisfaction were in vain. His feigned
light sleep and benign smile, signs of *his* sexual repletion,
studiously ignored.

He was made sorrowfully aware that there was un-
finished business, the completion of which he was
required to play some central part in.

Ten minutes later, she squeezed his hand and murmured, 'Goodnight.' Eventually, they slept.

The next day, comforted, he felt more keenly than ever that he was in danger of falling apart. His life was like watching a film of himself. The events of the previous evening had no more actuality for him than anything else that had happened in the preceding week: alienation, detachment from reality, and an unsettling sense of *déjà vu* that went on for hours, sometimes half a day.

When would it end, he wondered? He knew one thing: he certainly shouldn't be supervising a murder inquiry; sending detectives out, using valuable resources and hugely expensive overtime man-hours; setting up lines of inquiry; commandeering computers and technical resources; pursuing a car that was in the area on the night of a killing, and may have been seen elsewhere on the night of another.

He monitored Presley's reactions to him and his handling of the case. True, Presley thought he was out on a limb on the connection between the different murders. But they'd often differed on cases in the past. There *was* disquiet on the ship, but the officers weren't yet storming the bridge. They were still some way from open mutiny. Or so he thought. But how reliable was his perception of the unfolding events, he asked himself in his frequent moments of anxiety.

He was certain that he should take some leave. But leave was like money. When you had it, you didn't know what to do with it or, like all the famously rich, immediately found that it wasn't what you wanted anyway.

The apparent heart's desire had a faulty valve and sent pop stars in search of the rainforest Indians instead of a clever riff. The Roddicks went looking for a face cream; Branson went fast in boats and planes; Bardot saved the animals; Ginger Baker rode to hounds; Daltrey farmed fish.

No, he couldn't take leave. What would he do? Sit at

home and watch daytime television? Lie horizontal on the sofa, watch Channel Four racing and think about her, how much he missed her, and how much he wanted her back?

Set up in a basement room at the station headquarters, a monitor and a VCR in front of them, Merson and Gilks ran the garage tapes through on fast forward. They had been specifically instructed not to do this, but it was *they* who were suffering the narcoleptic tedium of watching hundreds of hours of Shropshire garage forecourts on black and white, poor-definition tape.

They could tell the rush hours of the day as the traffic built up, and then slowed down again until lunch time. Business picked up again at about 4.30.

There were a few Volvo 340s and 360s: the model had picked up the dubious notoriety that had once belonged to the Austin Allegro: assume the worst from their invariably elderly drivers.

There was a white 244 and an estate car, but no blue saloon throughout the day of the Sugar murders. At 17.38.53 (would it never just be 'nearly twenty to six' again, Merson wondered) a young lad and his girlfriend drove off in their battered Escort without paying, the number plate visible as he did so.

The two young men had their eyes on the rows of pumps: leaded, unleaded, diesel, as the images flicked by. It was wearing on the eyes.

'Stop it,' said Merson suddenly, and pulled his feet down from the desk. 'Rewind it.'

Gilks put his finger on the rewind button on the remote control. It was images such as these, not long ago, that had made people laugh out loud. No one even grinned now: the notion was as jaded as polystyrene ceiling tiles.

Merson leaned towards the screen as the cars reversed up to the pumps. It was a busy time of day. The shuddering white figures in the top left-hand corner of the screen said 18.17.

Gilks watched impassively as the BMWs and Renaults and Rovers came back to the pumps as the tape was rewound. Merson took the handset from his colleague and hit the pause button.

Gilks looked at the cars at the pumps. 'So what?'

'Look behind,' said Merson, and pointed at the airline in the far corner of the picture. A man was crouched at the front wheel of a big dark Volvo. Merson moved the shaky image on, one frame at a time. The man moved to the rear tyre and checked it, then the far side of the car. As he inflated the tyres, his back was to the camera. Could he possibly be doing it on purpose? Or was he an innocent driver checking his tyres?

Merson edged the tape on, frame by frame. The driver got in, fastened his seat belt, and drew slowly away, out of camera. They waited for him to reappear, to draw up to the pumps. Other cars arrived. The figures in the top left-hand corner of the screen flicked on: 18.25; 18.30; 18.33. Nothing happened. They waited and waited.

They rewound the tape another quarter of an hour to see if they had missed the man at the pumps on their first viewing. Nothing.

'The cheeky bastard,' said Merson eventually. 'He's one of those tossers who does his tyres, and doesn't buy any bloody petrol.'

But they were both pleased. They had a little shaky something-nothing. And it just *might* be something.

10

The young men's professional sang-froid precluded their beaming openly, but there was a certain something about their demeanour as they sat together in the incident room that said they were definitely the pussies who had today's cream on their whiskers.

Kavanagh's notion of a killer or killers perpetrating apparently unrelated murders, an idea never embraced with much enthusiasm by most of the officers, had begun to wear perilously thin with his colleagues.

To lighten the tone of the log-jammed inquiry, he'd even got hold of a couple of videos of *Strangers on a Train*. A lot of jokes followed: someone pinned a mug-shot of a Farley Granger lookalike on the inspector's desk; they started following the tennis stories on the sports pages and clipping items for him.

The barracking had been good-natured, but barely disguised the feelings of many of the detectives that not only were they barking up the wrong tree, but they were probably in the wrong forest.

Now, Kavanagh stood out front, the initiative, for the time being at least, back with him. Presley leaned against the pillar by the side of the flip charts. Kavanagh began. 'OK, folks, Gilks and Merson have got something. It might not be a hill of beans, but it could be something. Over to you, Kev.'

Presley arched his back, and said, 'As part of the search for a vehicle which was definitely at the scene of the Wellington murders, and may have been' – he stole a quick glance towards his boss – 'around on the night of *our* killing, Detective Constables Gilks and Merson have been down on our colleagues' patch in West Mercia collecting garage surveillance tapes.

'Naturally, we had to clear all this with Mercia's Chief Constable. Their own DI in charge of the Wellington killings, Tom Bromage, is not absolutely convinced that there's a connection between their murders and ours, but was quite happy, as long as we were discreet and shared everything we got, for our lads to be on their turf. It was, at the worst, going to do no harm, and at best, if anything came of it, would save them lots of overtime.

'So, ploughing through this year's entries for the Garage Forecourt Oscars, this is what we've got.' He nodded to Rees at the back of the room, who flicked off the lights, and then played the video recording on the trolley-mounted video monitor.

When the couple of minutes of relevant tape had been played through he handed back to his boss. The lights came up and Kavanagh started. 'It *may* be nothing. But it's Wednesday, the 15th September, the day before they found the Sugars' bodies. The bloke's in a Volvo 244. The technical boys are doing what they can with a copy of it, trying to enhance the quality.

'They may be able to ascertain the colour of the car by repeating the filming with half a dozen different model colours and then comparing them with this, but it all takes for ever, and there are other factors involved, like the age and wear and deterioration of this tape, compared with the one they use, and the amount of wear on the tape heads when this was recorded, but they're doing what they can for us.'

Using the handset, he froze the frame of the figure kneeling at his tyres. 'It's difficult to see much of the bloke. They're doing some estimates through reconstructions

71

using models of similar sizes to try and get his height and weight.

'He's thin and tall and wearing a jacket and jeans, quite conventionally dressed, boots rather than shoes, could be suede, no shine or reflection.

'As I say, it might be nothing, but it might be the break we're looking for. It's the right car, at the right time.

'Finally, we've got something from the SOCO people. They've isolated part of a footprint in Sugar's garage that's neither his nor his wife's. Terry Sugar was a dainty soul (pun intended), size seven. This is a size ten, right foot. It's a casual shoe, or desert boot, not a trainer, some sort of welted sole. They're working on that.

'It's recent, but it's still a long shot. Being a dope head, there may be all sorts of lowlifers coming and going scoring a bit of NHS smack or methadone. But it's something.

'Anyway, let's hear it for Merson and Gilks. The boys done good, and it *could* come to something.' There was some mock cheering and jeering as the men acknowledged their boss's plaudits.

Presley took over again. 'Any questions on that before we go on to the stuff we've been feeding in for the correlations on murders and victims?'

'What about the video cameras on the motorway? Can't we pick up the driver and his car on those?'

'Good question, Reeder. Unfortunately, they haven't got them on the M54. It's a bit primitive up there; England's rural motorway. Goes from somewhere to nowhere: no services, no petrol, no food. It's like things used to be. If it doesn't work, they can close it down and open it again as a museum. Anyway, no video cameras. Part of the government's cutbacks, I suppose.

'We've been running the stuff on the M6 that joins it near junction ten, but there's so much, it's taking for ever. But we're working on it. Anything else?'

There were no further questions. 'The other side to the inquiry is feeding in everything on the victims and the

72

murders to try and find any correlation. Both male victims, John Lacey and Terry Sugar, were in their mid-forties. Jeanette Sugar was a couple of years younger. Methods of killing, as we know, couldn't have been more different.

'Both murders were on Wednesday evenings, around about the same time. And yes, thanks to our own Patrick Moore, stargazer Detective Constable Tim Youle, it has been pointed out that they were within a day or two of a new moon.'

Immediate barracking and whistling followed. Presley held up his hands for quiet, but smiled at the notion that the phases of the moon were likely to have any bearing on the murders in hand.

When quiet had returned he continued: 'Tim says that it's not that the guy's a werewolf or a cloven-footer or anything, it's just that there's some folk who, well, are prone to certain kinds of behaviour, tend to be more susceptible to the moon's influence. Have I got it right, Tim?'

Youle acknowledged the sergeant's attempt at summarizing his knowledge of lunar influences: an increase in civil unrest, instability in prisons and mental homes; the silent power of the ocean's tides.

Young Donna Moss, on her first major inquiry, expressing the thoughts of many of the men and women in the room said, 'The differences are more significant than the similarities, surely?'

'Go on,' said Presley.

'The one man's an art teacher: middle class, professional; the other's a smack addict, a street trader. One's stabbed; the others are forced into a car and gassed. The one guy has a grown-up child; the other couple are childless. The Sugars live in Wellington, Shropshire; Lacey in a Birmingham suburb. The one guy's got a bit in the bank; the other one's living in a rented flat, has been for years. Shall I go on?'

Kavanagh stepped forward. He knew he was in danger

73

of losing the initiative. He'd thought the sighting of the car might swing things back his way. They were unimpressed. He was fulfilling his own prophecy, making the 'facts' fit his hunch-based hypothesis.

'Look, I'll say what I've said before. The last year for which we've got figures, there were seven hundred and twenty-six homicides. Half of those were killed in arguments or fights. Half of the female victims were killed by the bloke they were involved with. Most of the deaths were of children aged under one year. Put it another way, the "no suspect" victim was involved in only eleven per cent of the killings; of these, most were manslaughters. You can count the "no-obvious-suspect" murders on the fingers of one hand.

'Put those figures against the *apparently* motiveless murders, committed within forty miles of one another, on the same night of the week and within just four weeks of each other. Plus, there's a better than evens possibility there's a Volvo car connection. Add all that together and there's more of a link than Donna and the rest of you are suggesting.'

There was a polite but recalcitrant silence in the room. The video recorder's green figures flicked relentlessly on and off. The inquiry was in the balance. Kavanagh only just believed in what he was doing himself.

'We're sticking with it. We'll wait on the forensic and the video enhancement. We're digging further back into the victims' backgrounds, and we've got a couple of things to follow up from the TV show: someone who reckoned he'd got something on Sugar that Mercia have checked out, but we'll have a look, too.'

'And if nothing comes up?' said DC Denny.

'Maybe there'll be another "unexplained", and maybe there'll be the other half of a size ten at the scene. I dunno,' said the inspector. 'Stick with it. For now at least.'

'Sir,' said Tim Youle.

'Youle?' said Kavanagh.

'It's a full moon next Saturday. If we're logging un-explaineds, it might be a good idea for us to watch that day or two with particular care.'

'Sure,' said Kavanagh. 'Sure.'

11

The Sugars had died intestate.

Terry and Jeanette Sugar did have surviving relatives. But her aged mother was in a nursing home in Dawley, suffering from Alzheimer's disease and on a remorseless slide into oblivion.

On her daughter's weekly visits, they would sit together, and her mother would speak her garbled sentences, and often ask Jeanette when she, her daughter who was sitting beside her, bony hand enclosed in hers, was coming.

'I'm here, Mum. I *am* Jeanette. I'm here now, with you.'

Her mother would look about her and say nothing. A few minutes later, she would say, 'Our Jean's coming today. Is she here yet?'

And so it went on. 'Second childishness . . . mere oblivion.'

The 74-year-old would certainly be unable to comprehend the death of her only daughter.

Terry Sugar had a distant cousin living in the south of the country, in East Grinstead. The two men hadn't been in touch for over thirty years.

There was a flicker of avarice when the combined wit of the police, National Insurance office and the solicitor appointed to deal with their 'estate' tracked the man down to his home in Sussex. But any pecuniary interest quickly evaporated as the macabre nature of the deceased's death and his drug-dependent lifestyle was outlined to Sugar's corpulent cousin.

Reginald Sugar made it absolutely clear that he wanted nothing whatsoever to do with this part of his family. 'I'm a businessman. You saw the vans outside; I'm in central heating. It's taken me over twenty years to get this far. I employ a dozen blokes, an accountant, a secretary and a part-time wages clerk. How do you think it'd look in the local papers if this came out? I don't want anything to do with drugs and murder. I just can't afford it.' The man had a point.

The Sugars' solicitor communicated this to the local council, who proceeded with the funeral of the couple as soon as the police and the coroner had released the bodies.

An open verdict was recorded, and the ground-floor flat in the Victorian terraced house in Newport Road was secured against vandals and squatters pending its emptying and eventual reletting.

Going through the personal effects and belongings of any deceased person was a sobering task, and one that usually fell to council employees when no next of kin or beneficiary could be found to undertake it.

However, if the deaths were being treated as suspicious, it was police officers who had the unenviable job of filling thick plastic sacks with the detritus of a lifetime: photographs, letters, books, diaries, china and linen, pyjamas and bathing costumes, socks and underwear.

DI Tom Bromage's West Mercia force had already conducted a fruitless trawl through the couple's belongings in their search for clues to the deaths.

With his Shropshire colleague's reluctant permission, Kavanagh now sent in four of his own officers to see if they could discover anything that their colleagues had failed to.

'I want them to check everything, and I mean *everything*,' Kavanagh said sternly to Presley. 'We've only got one shot at this before the flat is closed down and their stuff's disposed of. It's got to be thorough. Tell them not to ignore anything that might be of any help, anything that doesn't make sense or looks odd. Anything: all right?'

'Sure,' said Presley. He flicked his eyes up to the forty pounds pinned to the notice board and flashed his boss a quick smile. 'Anything at all, Frank.'

DC Tim Youle sat at the little oak bureau and leafed through the letters and documents in the drawers there. Terry and Jeanette Sugar had not been great correspondents: there were letters from the council about window repairs and rent arrears; council tax demands; home contents insurance pitches and book club offers.

Perched on the arm of the moquette sofa, Youle read every letter as if, at some point, out of the humdrum contents, might lurch a name or a phrase, something, anything, that might throw light on the reasons for the deaths of the former occupants of the flat.

Two hours later, the drawers were empty, their contents stuffed into the plastic bag between his legs, and Tim Youle was still in his darkness.

Terry Sugar had been one of any number of prisoners who start doing education courses inside. He was bright, had the quick wit of the street trader that he was, and which might, in other circumstances, have conferred upon him a very different life.

He had started the Open University Arts Foundation course when he was doing nine months in Stafford in the mid-eighties for handling stolen goods.

Lots of prisoners dabbled with training inside; it passed their time and bestowed privileges. And, while smuggling hacksaw blades into prisons in birthday cakes to facilitate prisoners' escapes was considered very bad form, midlife sociology lecturers becoming romantically involved with their prisoner tutees was, if not the norm, by no means unusual.

There were, it appeared, women everywhere (men too, presumably, down the road at Holloway or wherever), who found a vicarious pleasure in this rough trade, thrilled to talk of heists and blaggings across prison tables, an hors d'oeuvre to more conventional sweet nothings on conjugal pillows.

Of course, most prisoners ceased their work on these, and any other, courses, as soon as they crossed the threshold of the prison gates. But a few, most famously the Jimmy Boyles and John McVicars, premier-league gangsters with tough, Barlinnie pedigrees, were accorded the ultimate accolade, the Prix Goncourt of prison celebrity: they made a page in the tabloids as they emerged with not only a university degree, but a sociologist/philosopher wife as well.

Detective Constable Andy Reeder, halfway through his own Open University law degree, was assigned the job of ploughing through Sugar's TMAs and assignments, and the associated computer-generated correspondence that had such a wearisome familiarity about it.

Reeder often told his friends: There's no need to phone Samaritans or join book clubs or send for free offers to newspapers. If you're lonely enrol for an OU course: never a day passes without a brown envelope dropping through your letter box with course information, counselling, assignments or student magazines.

Mindful of his instructions to be thorough, while DC Youle and DC Moss went through wardrobes and dressers and cabinets, Reeder opened the buff folders and glanced at the essays there: Shakespeare; T. S. Eliot; Auden; Gombrich's *Story of Art*. He scanned the letters from Milton Keynes with their details about examinations and essays and summer school arrangements for 1985.

DC Denny sat in the front room and went through the man's dark blue address book. She stuck a leaf of paper in the 'M's': entered after his GP's name, Dr Meriden, and his telephone number, and before Movies-in, a Wellington video rental store, was the enigmatic entry MND (SC) and a Shrewsbury code and number.

Back at the station, while Kavanagh was ensconced with the chief superintendent, and putting as favourable a gloss as he could on the scant progress being made on the inquiry, Youle, Moss, Reeder and Denny briefed Presley on the blank that *they* had drawn at the Sugars' flat.

Finally, Denny showed the sergeant the peculiar entry in Sugar's address book.

The dialling tone picked up and the phone began to ring. Three; four. When she was at home, and the phone caught her in the lavatory or the shower or down the garden, Denny always counted the double rings. Three; four; the pessimistic caller was considering one's not being there. Five; impatient contacts might hang up. Six; lots of people put the phone down. Seven or eight; all but the most persistent gave up.

The phone rang on; seven; eight. *They* were police. Nine; ten. This was work. They were paid for this. She let it ring on. The men around her had lost interest.

They were like the people who start to drift away from the ground, their team beaten. Eleven . . . suddenly the receiver was picked up.

'Hello,' said Denny.

It's injury time, but a faintly promising move has begun down the wing. Of course, the cross will be too long, or the fullback's tackle sweet, or the referee's whistle will blow, but they turn anyway, and wait. Presley and Youle and Reeder sauntered back towards the desk as she spoke.

'Hello?' said Denny again.

'Hello,' said the voice at the other end.

She raised her severely plucked eyebrows at her colleagues, and repeated, 'Hello, who is this, please?'

The sound of the receiver being clunked from one hand to another. 'Hello,' said a different, louder, more confident voice. 'This is Lianne.' Laughter. Excited, childish, playful laughter.

Denny could think of nothing to say. 'What's your friend's name, Lianne?'

'Jane,' came the unembellished answer.

'Where are you?' said the DC.

The laughter became hysterical.

When it subsided, she asked again, 'Where are you speaking to me from, Lianne?'

'The Precinct.'

'The Precinct? Where's that?'

'In Shewsbury.' (The 'r' had been dropped.)

'What are you doing there, Lianne?'

'Shopping.'

'Is it a public phone? A call box?'

'Yes. It was ringing so we answered it,' she said defensively.

'It's all right. You haven't done anything wrong,' Denny reassured her. 'Thank you, Lianne. Goodbye,' and she replaced the receiver.

'What do you reckon?' asked Presley.

'Sugar spoke to MND (SC) at a public call box in Shrewsbury. Maybe the person didn't have a phone? Or maybe they wanted to speak to the caller secretly, away from their own home. Who knows?' said Denny. 'Does anybody remember when itemized bills came in?' she continued.

'Check with BT,' said Presley. 'I think it was three or four years ago. But get them to send you copies of the Sugars' bills going back as far as they can.'

'It's not much of an anagram. No vowel,' said Reeder, as he played with the letters on his pad. 'They must stand for something. It *is* vaguely familiar.'

'Give the video store a ring,' said Presley to DC Youle.

'What for?' said the DC to his boss. 'You want to see a film?'

'Ask them when Sugar joined. You have to be a member, don't you? If we see when he joined, assuming he fills in his address book like everyone else in the world, we'll at least know that he *knew* MND (SC) before that time.

81

'And then call Dr Meriden or whatever he's called and see how long Sugar was registered with him. It'll give us a couple of dates within which we'll at least know that he must've met the initials person. It's not great, but it might be something.'

While Denny contacted British Telecom, Youle got through to the Asian owner of the Wellington video store.

The man was suspicious. Didn't understand what it was they wanted to 'clarify a point' about, doubted that they were the police. He knew of the Sugars' violent deaths, everyone in the little Shropshire town did.

Carrying his portable phone with him, he peered hopelessly out of his front window, thought it must be a practical joke. But he was a serious man, a man with few friends, who worked long hours and didn't really *know* about practical jokes, except for the ones that he saw played in the films that ran on the video recorder all day long in his shop. The man they were asking about *had* died. It had been in the *Shropshire Star*. Maybe it *was* the police.

He tapped Sugar's name into the grubby computer on the counter. Up came his address, telephone and membership number. 'He joined in April 1987,' said the man. 'Is that all?'

'Thank you,' said DC Youle, and put down the phone.

Denny tore off the faxes as they came in. When the machine had stopped its regurgitation, she came and reported to her colleagues. 'Itemized came in in Shropshire in 1990. There's nothing to our Shrewsbury call-box number between then and the latest bill. These are their bills for the last ten years though.' And after a pause, 'Eerie, isn't it, all that information logged away, just like that.'

'Do they tell us anything?' said Presley, ignoring the youngster's naïve observation.

'They're for very similar amounts,' said the DC. 'Except for one, which is nearly twice as much as the others. It's the only bleep.'

82

'Any ideas?' said Presley.

'None,' said Denny, wondering if this was some sort of Socratic dialogue, the unravelling of which the wise sergeant would reveal in the course of his peripatetic questioning.

'Which quarter?' he asked.

Denny leafed through the sheaf of faxed bills.

'Autumn. Dated October 1985. It's the bill for the period July to September '85.'

'So, what did you say, Tim, he's been registered with his doctor for twelve years? He's been a member of the video rental shop since '87. So he got to know MND between '81 and '87, which at least coincides with a heavy bill in '85.'

'Five years,' scoffed Denny. 'It's not enough, nowhere near. We can't link a big bill with that person just on that basis.'

'No, of course we can't,' said Presley. 'But it's an acorn, and at the moment I'll settle for that.'

Reeder stood in the doorway at the far end of the room and said,

'For aught that ever I could read,
Could ever hear by tale or history,
The course of true love never did run smooth.'

'What the fucking hell's up with you?' said the insouciant sergeant.

Reeder ignored his boss, walked to the blackboard and printed the words: *Midsummer Night's Dream*.

'Are you all right?' said Presley, his patience with the constable's performance wearing thin.

Reeder picked up the blackboard eraser and deleted the letters that followed the initials of each word. All that remained on the board was 'M' . . . 'N' . . . 'D'.

'Nice one, Andy. *Midsummer Night's Dream*. Shakespeare

play. So what? What does it mean? And what about the SC on the end? Where's that gone?'

'I *knew* I knew those letters. I've done the play myself. Everyone does it on the Arts Foundation course. It's the set text. I've abbreviated it every time I've taken tutorial notes or written a draft essay on it. I knew it rang a bell.'

'So, what do you reckon, then?' said Presley.

'Sugar went to OU summer school at Keele in 1985. I reckon he met someone there, had an affair with them, and he's entered her in his address book as MND . . . *Midsummer Night's Dream*.' He paused, and added conspiratorially, 'It's *A Midsummer Night's Dream*, actually . . .'

'Maybe it was!' interrupted Presley.

'And I bet if we check it out, we'll find there was someone there at the same time, with the initials SC,' said Reeder.

'Good work, Andy. So what now?'

'I thought maybe Denny and I might go down to Milton Keynes and see how many SCs were at Keele that summer.'

12

They didn't have to wait for Saturday evening's full moon. Adam Curtiss was on his way to see his mother in Leamington Spa on the late Friday afternoon train. His body was found beside the track the following morning. He had fallen from the inter-city from London between Rugby and Coventry. It had probably been dark. The clocks had gone back only the previous weekend. British summer time was over.

British Rail launched an immediate inquiry; they had been losing too many passengers falling from trains in recent months, and questions were being asked in the House about the effects of financial cutbacks and the deleterious effect they might be having on passenger safety. There were a lot of Labour Party mutterings about cutting corners as the next big target was softened up for privatization.

The police were involved at an early stage. The man was sober and had sat near other people on the train who had noticed nothing extraordinary about his behaviour. He had left his jacket, overnight bag and book on his seat as he went, they assumed, to the buffet car or the lavatory.

He didn't return and, with customary English reserve, though each of them was aware of the gap in their silent midst, they said nothing to one another about the continued absence of their fellow passenger.

At Birmingham, with the train disembarked, it fell to

a cleaner to gather his things and deposit them at Lost Property.

His mother waited for him, assumed the train had been delayed, and turned the heat down on the tarka dahl, vegetable curry and rice, that she had made for him. By ten o'clock, two hours after he was due, she was so concerned that she telephoned Birmingham's New Street station.

The train had arrived, on time. She telephoned his little flat in Finsbury Park. There was no answer. Adam was a thoughtful and reliable man, entirely dependable. She had no idea what could have happened to him.

Very early the next morning, she telephoned the police in London. They told her not to worry, took the details about her son and sent a car to his address, just one of many, siren blaring and blue lights flashing, that split the city's morning traffic every day.

At about the same time, hurtling past the spot on her way to work, Curtiss's body was spotted by a passenger. The woman felt very diffident and rather foolish but, agitated beyond endurance, the train getting further and further from the spot, she eventually shared the shocking news with a fellow commuter.

The two women walked half the length of the train before they found the guard and told him that one of them was sure she had seen a body lying at the foot of the embankment.

As one of the 'unexplained' deaths that were being monitored with even more rigour than usual, the news soon came through to Kavanagh's team. Was it just another fall from a train, or was there more to it?

The man was travelling alone; there was no possibility of drunken joshing or horseplay. Had he committed suicide? Had the door flown open and sucked the man out as he went to the lavatory? Had it been poorly secured? Had Curtiss leaned against it, and fallen to his death?

Kavanagh dispatched pathologist Dr Khaliq to the Warwickshire mortuary where the body lay.

The same week, there was a hit-and-run in Cumbria: accident and panic? A body hauled from the Thames; a tramp kicked to death near King's Cross; a middle-aged homosexual, an accountant who built model boats, bludgeoned to death in his flat in Whitechapel.

They were all long shots, but they were 'unexplaineds', 'AWMs' as they'd come to be known on the inquiry: 'apparently without motives'. All the information was fed in, cross-referenced and screened for connections.

The tramp was ruled out: according to the unreliable meths and wino witnesses, his was a cheap life extinguished by a gang of skinhead Nazis, fired up on strong lager and a basement racist gig by a bunch of Screwdriver clones.

The gay man, according to the only neighbours who were prepared to talk to the police, had almost certainly died at the hands of one of the many rent boys who visited the man. But there was no clear evidence, and he stayed in the Kavanagh file.

The Thames body was a mystery, but the river police pulled out three dozen corpses a year, and the likelihood was that this was just another tragic soul who would probably never even be correlated with his name on the Missing Persons File.

The list ran into thousands and thousands of names, and they were only the tip of the iceberg: thousands more left homes where no one cared for their fate sufficiently to even register them as missing.

That weekend, a man fell to his death from the Severn Bridge. The video cameras mounted on the bridge established that he was alone when he climbed the unforgiving metal and plunged into the swirling brown water two hundred feet below.

The train death was interesting, but there had been a

rash of these accidents recently, and this itself cast doubt on foul play. However, they'd look closely at Mr Curtiss's demise, even as the British Rail Transport Police inquiry and its technical division got on with their investigations.

Notwithstanding the possible sightings of a Volvo near the scene of both murders, Kavanagh's theory of linked killings was looking increasingly flimsy. If there *had* to be another death, he'd been hoping that that death could be used as the glue to bring the others together. Apart from its happening a day before the full moon, Adam Curtiss's demise had almost no similarities with the other killings.

A drug-using, petty-criminal street trader; a middle class, law-abiding teacher, and now a male nurse on the wards of a London psychiatric hospital.

The only common denominator was the fact that they had all died suspicious or violent deaths recently.

'Which is exactly where we started a month ago,' said Presley.

'Yes,' replied Kavanagh, as he scrolled the masses of information before him on the computer screen. 'At least we have another death which, if it was murder, was made to look like suicide.'

'Maybe it *was* suicide,' said Presley, glancing at his twenty-pound note pinned to the notice board.

'But if it was a murder, and the Sugars, too, why not just kill them?' rejoined Kavanagh.

'I suppose it buys the "killer" some time. Mixes it up for us, at least for a bit. We wouldn't be onto him for a while. If Curtiss's death *is* murder, he might have got away with it; it wouldn't normally be looked at this closely. He doesn't know we're logging all suspicious deaths for a tie-up.'

'Curtiss may not be involved with the other two,' reasoned Kavanagh, 'I agree, but he wasn't a suicide case. He was a Buddhist, for Christ's sake. Meditation and chanting, weeks away in silent Northumbria. Buddhists don't kill themselves, El. The eightfold path and all that. Life is suffering . . .'

'Sounds like a good reason for topping yourself,' said Presley, unimpressed by his boss's apparent familiarity with Eastern theology. 'Also, he did work in a nuthouse. You know, preaching to the converted and all that. Aren't all social workers ex-dope heads or something, poachers turned gamekeepers? They're unstable people, Frank.'

'Come on, Elvis, the guy was going home to see his mother. He'd phoned her that morning from work. He had a return ticket. He didn't kill himself. Anyway, you'd have to be mad to use a train. It's horrible, and you're not certain. People who use trains are disturbed.'

'You're not kidding,' said Presley. 'The crowding's terrible, and they're never on time!'

Kavanagh managed a smile at his colleague's grim humour.

The door opened and Khaliq came in.

'Well?' said Kavanagh, eschewing formal greetings.

'Sorry?' said the doctor, abstruse.

'What's the weather forecast, doctor?' said Kavanagh.

Khaliq played him a straight bat. 'Rain in the Midlands, probably before dawn . . .'

'Khaliq, what about Curtiss, please?'

'Injuries consistent with multiple trauma as a result of falling, or being ejected from, a train travelling at high speed. It's been dry. The ground was very hard there, it's a sheltered spot, and as well as the initial impact, the fall to the bottom of the embankment, at an angle of some forty-five degrees, is a good thirty feet.' He paused.

'Was he pushed?' said Presley.

'Impossible to say. Impossible for *me* to say. Forensic might help you with the door, the handle, the glass, for prints, but the rail police are all over that, and then your Coventry colleagues will no doubt want to have a go. I doubt there'll be much for you to look at by the time our people get to see it.

'And anyway,' he added. 'If I was going to kill somebody by pushing them out of a train, I'd wear gloves. Wouldn't you?'

The inspector ignored the supercilious sarcasm. 'Booze? Drugs?' he said hopelessly.

'Nothing. Last meal, a light lunch. No drink or drugs, not even traces. He didn't drink or smoke. Last clean-living man in the Western world.'

'Anything else?' asked Kavanagh.

'Nothing material, I'm afraid,' said Khaliq. 'I'll put it all in writing, let you have it by lunch time tomorrow. OK?'

'Sure. Thanks.' Kavanagh pointed to the window and the early-evening Saturday sky, a pink tinge lying across the last of the light. '"Red sky at night, shepherd's delight," my old man always used to say,' said the inspector.

'Umm,' said Khaliq, the first few drops of rain starting to fall on the black glass. 'What was it your father did for a living, Inspector?'

The information on the screen rolled up and disappeared with neither man looking at it consciously.

They tapped in the password and keyed into the Coventry force's newly compiled file on Adam Curtiss. His birth date, schooling, career and addresses; next of kin, driving-licence number, bank accounts and credit-card limits tripped up the screen. It made unremarkable reading.

'What's that?' said Presley, leaning forward.

'What?'

'There,' said the sergeant. 'What's that about Curtiss being arrested in Cardiff?'

Kavanagh took his finger from the scroll key. The green letters shimmered there. *Adam Curtiss, arrested Cardiff, 1974. Disturbing the peace. Bound over.*

'So what?' said the inspector.

'Didn't Lacey spend some time in Cardiff? A postgraduate degree, or something?' said Presley.

Kavanagh tapped in a few letters. The computer instantly flashed up a 'No match found. Try again' message.

Both men looked at the screen. The thing about computers was that they were never wrong. They said, 'Try again,' but when you did, the message always came back the same; they were unforgiving.

Kavanagh swung his legs down from the desk. 'You're right though, El. I'm sure he did,' said the inspector. 'Judith Lacey told us.'

They keyed into the file on Lacey. The text rolled away on the screen: schooling; contacts; family; student holiday jobs; NUT membership; passport numbers; holidays, and then: *1974/5 Post Graduate Degree; MA. Caerdydd.*

'What the fuck's *Caerdydd*?' said Presley.

Kavanagh grinned. 'Bloody Cardiff in Welsh. Political correctness bilingual bollocks. But the fucking computer doesn't understand. Doesn't match Caerdydd with Cardiff, doesn't tell us that two men who are now dead . . . have died violent deaths within a few weeks of each other . . . were *both* in Cardiff in 1974. Good man, Elvis.'

'Don't get excited, Frank, it's probably nothing.'

'Yes, I'm sure you're right, but at least it's *something* nothing!' said the inspector.

13

Mrs Curtiss must have been one of the very few readers of the *Morning Star* in the village of Claverdon, a couple of miles outside Leamington Spa. In fact, she may have been its only reader in rural Warwickshire. Frank Kavanagh hadn't seen the paper for years; wasn't even sure that he knew that it was still published. Hadn't the Cold War ended? Weren't there now lots of horrible little hot wars instead?

Kavanagh and his estranged wife had worried about the Holocaust, the same as the rest of their contemporaries, but at least, until the big one went off, and they all retreated to their cellars and caught up on Salman Rushdie and Stephen Hawking (until they got too ill to read anything at all), there *was* peace in those huge, dark, foreign countries.

Nowadays, the horror stories from former Soviet satellites and ex-colonial African countries were legion as they tore one another apart with a scale and savagery that was impossible to comprehend.

So, what was the *Morning Star*'s line, he wondered? Were they still waiting for the revolution? Where did the editor stand on the changes in the Eastern bloc and the all of the Berlin Wall when for a few moments it looked, like the Band Aid concerts before them, as if people really *could* change the world?

It had now been some days since the discovery of her son's body, and Ruth Curtiss had been interviewed by both British Rail Transport Police and the local CID, as well as suffering the ordeal of formally identifying her son.

She was a very fit woman, in her late seventies, and had short, grey hair, carried no spare flesh, was wiry, upright and brisk. Family and friends had supported her through the first days of her loss, but she was an independent woman and, in truth, by only the second day, she couldn't wait for the neighbours and Party friends and, most of all, her sister from Stratford-upon-Avon, to go home.

Ruth Curtiss was not without emotion; on the contrary, she mourned her only son's death deeply. But she was wholly inadequate when it came to rehearsing those feelings to others. However, with virtually all other topics of conversation suspended, her withdrawal left awkward silences that her visitors felt obliged to fill.

Now, nearly a week after her son's death, what she actually wanted, more than anything, was to be left alone. She felt the need to establish once more her routines: solitary breakfast, walking her mongrel dog, listening to *Today* on Radio Four. It wouldn't bring Adam back; but neither would the unnatural silence in her flat, which seemed to be the only alternative to the conspiratorial talk of friends and relatives in the kitchen, from which she, the subject of that talk, was rigorously excluded.

No Mother Teresa of the British Communist Party, she was, nevertheless, a pragmatist who lived an austere, an almost spartan life. Her political beliefs were the rock upon which she had built it, and it was the bulwark against all the ordeals that she had faced in that life.

Above the mantelpiece was a little bronze bust of Lenin. Kavanagh stroked the man's head with the back of his index finger as he said, pointing to that day's *Morning Star*, 'Does it still have the appeal for funds every day?'

'Yes, every day,' she replied phlegmatically. 'I'm afraid the Party needs money more than ever. Falling membership, the recession. Things are hard at present. But they'll change. It's just a cycle. It's all there in Marx. You can't keep producing goods that people don't need. And cheaper and cheaper goods at that, so that ultimately people's standard of living is driven down and down as even more oppressed labour markets are exploited.'

Hers was an evangelic faith: there was nothing that couldn't be answered by the 'good books' that filled the shelves and crowded all the surfaces in her little sitting-room.

Kavanagh was not hostile to notions of socialist collectivism, but he had always been cynical about an economy which left the average Russian more likely to see a cosmonaut float by in the night sky than to find a banana in the shops of Leningrad. But he knew, of course, that not everyone judged society's progress according to the availability of bananas and he remained silent during Mrs Curtiss's party political broadcast.

She made tea, and the three of them sat at her dining table which overlooked the neatly planted area in front of her second-floor flat. 'My sister is staying with me at the moment, but she's gone to the shops. It's about Adam's death, of course?'

'Yes,' said Kavanagh, 'I'm afraid so.'

'It's all right. I can cope, and I can talk, but I do hope that one day you will find out what really happened.'

'We'll certainly do our best,' volunteered Kavanagh. 'We're not convinced about the door coming open. As you know, British Rail are conducting their own investigations into that. But we need to make our own inquiries, to satisfy ourselves that there was no . . .'

'Foul play?' she offered.

'Quite,' said the policeman.

'Adam didn't take his life. I know that. He had an entirely different approach to life from me. He wouldn't have said so, he was too kind, but he thought all my politics were a waste of time. He believed only in the inner, spiritual search. Hence his Buddhism.'

'I see,' said the inspector. 'And was he happy?'

'"Happy"?' she reiterated. 'In this world? He was content; resigned, perhaps, would be a better word.'

'And that's why you say he would have been unlikely to . . . have taken his own life?'

'Buddhists believe that life is founded on suffering, that there are endless rebirths until one achieves a state of grace, nirvana, when one is released from the cycle of pain and death and rebirth. It's an interesting notion.' She leaned down and stroked the dog that lay quietly at her feet. 'I don't believe it, of course. Suffering *is* part of the human condition, but the intervention required to alleviate it is not divine. All that *is* required is for employers to share the fruits of their workers' toil equally amongst them, and for worker not to turn against worker.'

She spoke in quiet tones of patient exasperation, the truth of her conviction so clear as to be blindingly obvious. She poured the two policemen more tea, offered them Co-op digestive biscuits, and went through to the kitchen to refill the pot.

'Do you know of anyone who might have wished your son any harm, Mrs Curtiss?' said Kavanagh, as she stood at the doorway waiting for the kettle to boil.

'No one. He led a very quiet life. Worked at the hospital. Went to the temple for meditation three times a week. He read a lot, mostly religious and spiritual texts, and listened to the radio. He didn't really meet many people, apart from at work. I don't think he had any enemies. He was a gentle, serious, kindly person.'

Presley was intrigued. 'How long had he been involved with the Buddhism?' he asked, the use of the definite article relegating the man's spiritual quest to the level of a hobby.

'About fifteen years.'

'And before then?' said Kavanagh, faintly suspicious of the motives of people who embraced religion, suspecting skeletons in well-concealed cupboards.

'He had always been a quiet, introspective kind of person, but before that, he did see friends, had a girlfriend or two, and did all those things that people did in the seventies.'

'What sort of things?' asked the sergeant.

'I think he experimented with drugs, that kind of thing.'

When she took her seat at the table again, Kavanagh said, 'We have four unexplained deaths on our files at the moment, Mrs Curtiss. They are "unexplained" in the sense that they are apparently motiveless, but they don't appear to be the result of random attacks. We're trying to establish whether there might be any connection between these deaths that we haven't yet discovered.

'One of the other men who died in suspicious circumstances spent some time in Cardiff. I believe your son did, too. Wasn't he arrested there in the seventies?'

'Yes, he was,' she said proudly. 'It was a march in support of the miners. Between us we brought down a whole government. Cynics say that ordinary people can't change the course of history. But do you remember those days? Do you remember Vietnam? People driving in the daylight hours with their headlights on? Burning their draft cards in Washington? Marching in their thousands on Grosvenor Square? They *did* change the world.'

Kavanagh thought that Edward Heath had lost the vital propaganda war during the coal strike: the rights and wrongs of the dispute were immaterial to the outcome; the real battle was the one fought out beneath the media's spotlight glare. And he had *no* doubt that television news pictures had played a bigger part in the Americans' withdrawal from Vietnam than any number of people chanting outside the American Embassy.

He said nothing. If Ruth Curtiss believed that it was her son's arrest, and hundreds like it, that had finally forced the politicians' hands, so be it. Driving with headlights on had a kind of folksy charm, like yellow ribbons wrapped round trees, but he doubted its power to sway the hard men of the Republican Party.

'What we'd like to do, Mrs Curtiss, is get more background on your son's life from you, all the places that he visited, as many of his friends' and colleagues' and associates' names as possible. Places of work, where he drank or who he went out with, and then we can feed all of the material into the computer and see if it throws up any cross-references with the other deaths that we're looking at. Would that be all right?'

'Of course,' she said. 'Do you want us to do it now?'

'Yes, perhaps you could make a start. Sergeant Presley here will jot things down and then if you recall things that you've missed, he'll call round or you could give us a ring.'

He liked her. She was spunky. In her seventies, nearly eighty, she was fighting the good fight, would not be denied, did not waver in her belief that there was a world out there peopled with decent folk ready to embark on honest toil with an open heart.

She was the good guys, same as the folk down at the local church. You may not want to sing hymns, clap hands, clasp neighbours to you, but these people would do you good before they did you harm. What price a little proselytizing? They wouldn't steal your bag, rob your pension, rape your sister. The rest was academic.

She reminded him of his own elderly mother. She had been distraught about the break-up of his marriage. He'd even kept it from her for a while. His mother, the one with the womb-love, the deepest, most unconditional love, that nothing can supplant.

How often had he seen people put away for the most heinous crimes: child murders, dreadful sexual attacks, barbarity of every sort, and yet he had never once seen a mother desert her son, deny the monster at her side her love.

He resented Rachael as much for hurting his mother as

for what she had done to him. And yet he knew, of course, that it was his mother who was 'responsible' for himself, her own son: nature or nurture; environment or genes; one way or another, Frank Kavanagh was Rosemary Kavanagh incarnate.

And now *he* was separated; her daughter had never married; her second son, married young, was now divorced. The Kavanagh family fallout was complete.

There was no blame, no censure: his mother had had a hard life: not hard in the sense of little to eat, or having to wear thin, cheap shoes. But in the sense of life being hard for her to live. He saw it in her face. So much anxiety: anxious to be happy, to please, to feel others' suffering. The things that made it hard for her to be happy; easily, ordinarily happy, without fear of the snatching away of that happiness.

How difficult her uncompromising love had made it for those children, now grown men and women, mortgages to pay, lives to lead, marriages and friendships to fail in, again and again.

How ashamed they were of their own fallibilities.

Kavanagh loved her with a deep, resentful, unwholesome, claustrophobic love. They had become even closer since the break-up. She had stood by him, of course, for blood is blood. And he was her murderous child; pederast, paedophile or pimp.

But he resented her love, for he knew, without needing to articulate it, that it was *this* love that had always rendered his own a failure.

From Mrs Curtiss's home in Claverdon, he drove up through Solihull, into Birmingham and towards his estranged wife's flat on Stratford Road. He knew the address, but until today had detoured rather than pass it.

He thought about her virtually every waking moment; he woke to thoughts of her each day; his sleep was a thin veneer that lay over his consciousness and into which, at what seemed like every few minutes, images of her would break.

He went to bed drunk, but still woke several times each night, the slightest sound disturbing him. He tormented himself with thoughts that she was there; called out, knew that she had been at the door or the window, and might now be walking away.

He stopped his breathing and called out to her; lay without moving or sound, called again to the blackness, got up, went to both doors, looked down the empty pavement, was bitter that she was not there, knew she was somewhere else.

His imagination was in the ascendancy, the balance tipped; he didn't believe any reality of her life could be as skewering as his recurrent imaginings.

He wanted to turn away, but couldn't, he was being drawn down the busy street. On he went, towards her flat.

Two hundred yards away, he checked his rear-view mirror, saw that there was nothing close behind him, did a big U-turn and drove away towards his own house.

14

The two officers drove down to the Open University's headquarters at Milton Keynes and got into the records office with less difficulty than you can get into a First Division football match.

All the student records' information since the institution's inauguration twenty-four years earlier was logged on computers the size of small power stations.

The girl who accessed the files didn't even wear a white coat, certainly didn't look like a scientist. (What *did* a scientist look like?)

She was matter of fact about their inquiries, and gave the impression that, while it was something readily achieved, she could just as easily have told the two officers that their request was impossible to fulfil, quoting, had she wished, procedural or confidentiality rules, the need for a magistrate's warrant, or the Charter of the European Court of Human Rights.

Given that she was, albeit a little sullenly, acceding to their request, they maintained a discreet presence and stood aside as she glided around the floor on her chair and pushed the buttons that sent the memory-packed disks on their erratic stop/start spinning way.

There were several screens in front of her and she glanced from them to the piece of paper in her hand with Terry Sugar's details on it.

Eventually, his name came up: when he had enrolled; where; which course; tutors; personal tutor; essay and assignment marks; summer school; residence arrangements. It didn't say if he jerked off in room nineteen of Lindsay Hall in the summer of 1985 at Keele University, but there wasn't much else missing.

It really was an unequal struggle; criminals shouldn't have a chance these days. And yet, whether it was the blocked drains of homosexual killer Dennis Nilsen, or the out-of-date tax disc on the car of the so-called Yorkshire Ripper, it was often this kind of aberration which led to arrests.

Sugar was straightforward. They knew him, knew what to try and ascertain about him to flesh out his picture.

But MND (SC), the person whose initials appeared in his address book, and whose contact telephone number was a public call box in Shrewsbury, was harder.

From the roll of students, hundreds of thousands of them, people's names going back two and a half decades, they had to try and isolate any SCs. If they were lucky, they might then link her to a summer school in the mid-eighties at Keele.

It could be done. Yes, said the girl in her wheeled chair, but it would take some time, the best part of a day. She had other work to do as well. She would fax them the information through as soon as she had it.

The two officers left the red-brick building in Milton Keynes and joined the M1 for the journey up to Keele University in Staffordshire.

'I don't think I've quite got this,' said Kavanagh.

'Good. It makes a change, anyway,' said Presley.

'You're telling me Adam Curtiss goes to see his old mate in Cardiff?'

'For a miners' rally. Writes to him and asks if he can stay over for a day or two.'

'And Curtiss's mate . . . Jeff?'

'Jeff.'

101

'Jeff's missis falls for Curtiss and they have an affair?'

'Not straightaway. Nothing happens. It's all nods and winks between Curtiss and Jeff Clarke's missis, Sarah. Curtiss goes back to London, the husband doesn't suspect anything. Well, in a way, there isn't anything to suspect. Not really.'

'And then?'

'Then, about two weeks later, Sarah Clarke ups and goes to London.'

'Just like that?'

'Apparently; so Mrs Curtiss says. Called her "the bolter",' said Presley.

'"The bolter"?' repeated Kavanagh.

'It's from a book. Nancy Mitford. Don't you know it, Frank?'

'It rings a bell. Anyway, how long have you been reading Nancy Mitford?'

'I haven't. Mrs Curtiss told me. Mitford's sister was a Communist. Big anti-fascist or something. Another sister was married to Mosley though, Oswald Mosley.'

'OK, Kev. Can we get the history and literature later? So, Sarah Clarke fucks off to London.'

'To see Adam Curtiss. The Clarkes had got a little kid. She takes her too.'

'Good mother!'

'This Jeff's doing a teacher-training course. He comes home with his pile of marking and she's gone. Note on the mantelpiece job.'

'And?'

'And she phones, and they talk, and she says she needs a few days to sort out her feelings.'

'And her old man gets on the next train to London and kills them both?'

'No, he doesn't. It's the seventies, and he says, "You've got to decide what's right for you. Sort it out, as soon as you can."'

'You're having me on.'

102

'I'm not. That's what he says.'

'And?'

'And in two days' time he comes to London . . .'

'And kills her?'

'And takes her back. According to old Mrs Curtiss, there's this tense scene in her son's flat, with Sarah Clarke and her husband talking in one room, and then Sarah and Curtiss talking in another room, and then Curtiss and the husband talking in the kitchen, and the upshot is that she packs her bag and the Clarkes go back to Cardiff together.

'According to Curtiss's mother, her son was being "magnanimous"; the girl didn't want to go back, but Curtiss said she should. "It's Jeff you're married to, got a nipper by, and that's where you belong," he says.'

'Maybe he didn't fancy her,' said Kavanagh.

'Maybe he thought she was nuts,' replied Presley.

'Yes, maybe. Then what?'

'It didn't work out for the Clarkes. The Curtiss romance hadn't run its course, and the girl is still pining and things are all over the place. I should think he wasn't teaching very well, either! Anyway, they're going round in circles, and it's half term, so the husband, Jeff, he says, rather than *her* go away, and take the nipper and everything, *he*'ll go away for a few days and Adam Curtiss can come and be there for them to finally sort out what it is this woman wants.'

'You're kidding,' said Kavanagh calmly. 'Jeff Clarke leaves his own house to let his mate come and be with his wife?'

'You've got it, Frank. I'm telling you just what Curtiss's mother told me. She wasn't very proud, either, but she said that's the way it happened, and maybe things were different then.'

'Did Mrs Curtiss ever meet the girl?'

'Yes, she lived in London at that time and met her on her first visit. She said she liked her. Middle class, ex-military family. She'd made up her mind not to have

103

anything to do with her, but she said she was nice. Young, mixed up a bit, but "a sweet girl" is what she said.'

'She *sounds* sweet,' said Kavanagh. 'Go on. This is the worst story I've heard all day.'

'Well, the husband goes away, and amazingly, it works. Perhaps Jeff Clarke *did* know what he was doing. He's away for a few days, three or four, I think, and in that time, maybe the strange situation or the little girl around, whatever, the spark went out.

'When he comes back, Curtiss has gone, and Sarah Clarke and Adam Curtiss were never in contact again. At least that's what his mother says.'

Eventually Kavanagh asked, 'Did she say what happened to them, the girl and her husband?'

'She doesn't know.'

'And her son becomes a Buddhist. One day he's having it off with his mate's missis, the next he's picking up wood-lice so he doesn't kill them.'

'What you on about?' said Elvis. 'What's this about woodlice?'

'Karma, mate. Instant karma. John Lennon had a song about it: "Instant karma's gonna get you . . ."' sang Kavanagh, distinctly off key.

'What's karma got to do with anything?' said Presley.

'I'm just wondering if you have to wait until your *next* lifetime to pick up the tab on your misdeeds, or whether this lifetime'll do,' said the inspector.

'Fuck knows,' said Presley. 'But the good news is that her name's Sarah Clarke; *and* there's a Cardiff connection. John Lacey spent time in Cardiff doing a degree, and we think that Sugar had an affair with someone whose initials were SC.

'We've been looking for a connection and now it looks like we've got three. I hate losing money, don't you, Frank?'

15

'It's for you, Frank.' Presley held the receiver at arm's length, a cigarette in his mouth, and continued his conversation into the other phone.

It was difficult for cops not to parody themselves these days. The police college might as well lock the recruits in the TV lounge with two hundred episodes of *The Bill*. Its writers and producers knew more about police work than Chief Constables. And they had a better clear-up rate.

The inspector took the phone from Presley's outstretched hand. 'Hello, Kavanagh speaking.'

'Hello, Inspector.'

He knew the voice, but couldn't place it. He felt a little guilt and embarrassment, as if he should know it, and had been found out. He waited for her next words.

'This is Judith Lacey.'

'Ah, Mrs Lacey, I'm sorry, it's a poor line.'

She wasn't interested in the telephone lines, just said, 'I think you'd better come round.'

'Yes, of course. Now?' He glanced up at the Smith's electric on the wall with its green figures and ceaselessly sweeping hand. It was four in the afternoon.

'Yes, as soon as you can.'

'Of course; I'll be straight round.'

Although Kevin Presley's oft-remarked observation that 'Sex is all right, but not when you can do the real thing' always made Frank smile, onanism, for Kavanagh, was the sexual equivalent of a Chinese meal: it satisfied you for a while, but very soon . . .

As he drove out to the Laceys' suburban house in leafy Sutton Coldfield, he blushed to admit to himself that the voice on the phone belonged to the woman he had made love to in his imagination on several occasions since he had spoken to her at her husband's funeral.

In fact, since that day, the widow Judith Lacey, with her subtle allure, had even supplanted his former lover, Lucy Amis, in his lascivious thoughts in those most secret, dark and solitary moments.

Lucy Amis, with whom, to his considerable chagrin at the time, he had spent an illicit night three or four years into his marriage to Rachael.

Heartbroken at their separation and, by the most subtle employment of a scrawled extra kiss, or subliminally loaded word in the birthday and Christmas cards that she always sent, Lucy indicated, as clearly as was decently possible, that she was waiting patiently in the wings, understudy to the younger Rachael, the woman for whom she had been precipitately abandoned after two years of more or less contented cohabitation.

Ever vigilant, she had driven halfway across the country when Kavanagh had disingenuously mentioned to her on the telephone that he was alone at the family home, 'an urgent, pressing case', his wife still on holiday with her parents.

Four or five hours later, as they climbed into the bed in the guest room and she suffused him with the pent passion of the intervening years, she murmured the unremarkable words, 'My lust is just returning.'

At that moment, and at every moment since, when he chose to recall those prosaic words, they unfailingly acted as a clarion call to his nascent sexuality.

'I maintained it until Northampton,' she had continued breathlessly. 'And then it disappeared all the way up the M6. But now it's returning.'

This, as she unclasped her brassiere, and he nuzzled his head into the deep cleavage of that ample bosom.

The very thought of Lucy Amis hurtling across the country towards him, his self the subject of *her* sexual arousal, was a powerful aphrodisiac and his thoughts-erotic had gathered apace as he thrilled at the prospect of losing himself once more in the red hair and soft places of this Rubensesque woman.

(Had there ever, he wondered, been a woman in the history of the entire world who had monitored her salacious thoughts en route to *Birmingham*, observing their fading and finally flickering out on the ring road of Northampton?)

But now, since the tremor that had rocked his life sex, alone or with any other, was a troubled affair and even as his blood vessels filled in a kind of independent and non-aligned sexuality, he had to struggle to ignore the nation-state of his whole being.

Perhaps, from now on, it would be easier. Perhaps it was time to try again: he'd had enough Chinese meals. Now he wanted an English three-course dinner of a tryst, not just another oriental takeaway.

She opened the door and walked back into the sitting room, leaving him to follow. Her body swayed and rocked, not with self-conscious allure, but with the lack of it that comes with drink.

The oval, pale, Kashmiri carpet at the centre of the sitting-room floor was covered with paper and envelopes. There was a space in the centre where she had been sitting, and a bottle of gin close at hand. On the hearth were several empty Schweppes tonic water bottles. (Why did she buy the prohibitively expensive tiny size? Kavanagh wondered.)

The ashtrays were full of her half-smoked Silk Cut stubs.

'Drink?' she said.

'Do you have a whisky?' he asked.

He stood in front of the sofa, looking down at the detritus as she went through to the kitchen.

She came back with an unopened bottle of Bell's and a cut-glass tumbler.

'Anything with it?'

'No, this'll be fine,' he said.

She gestured for him to sit on the settee, and knelt down in her nest of letters. She lit a cigarette and the smoke sputtered out of her mouth as she spoke. 'You were right, Inspector. How did you know?'

'Right about what?' he said.

'He *had* had another affair.'

'Really?' said Kavanagh, barely surprised, given the evidence that lay about her on the floor.

'Not now,' she continued. 'Well, at least, I don't think so. But he had done.'

He poured himself a triple and leaned back into the cushions. What he was about to hear may or may not be material to the inquiry, but Kavanagh was a man who also had recently undergone major surgery: he wanted to show *his* scars, compare *his* stitches, talk about *his* operation, but only to someone who had also felt the surgeon's knife.

He had seen this woman in shock on the night of her husband's murder; in mourning at his funeral, and now she was in a volatile state of anger and hurt. It was a heady mixture. She looked as attractive as on the other occasions that he had seen her, just different: her eyes full of hurt and intense emotion. She looked as if she might cry at any moment.

She started abruptly, 'I was going through some of his things. It has to be done, I thought. I'll make a start.

'Joe's out. Gone to a rave or something. Up to no good, I'm quite sure, but they all go. What can you do?

'The clothes, the jackets, each one something particular, special. I'd done a couple of bin bags. It was about as bad as I had imagined, a bit worse perhaps. Lots of gin and cigarettes. I tried some music, but that was all too difficult, so I turned it off.

'I didn't want to handle any more of his clothes, it was upsetting me too much. His shoes in particular, I just couldn't pick them up. They had the shape of his foot so clearly.

'I was crying quite a lot by this time, just getting lower and lower, and so I said to myself, "This is stupid. Stop it."

'Anyway, I came in here, watched the TV for a bit and then wandered over to his desk and started to go through some of his papers.' She stopped as abruptly as she had begun. 'And here we are.'

'What exactly did you find?'

She swept her arm in front of her, gin and tonic spilling on the letters. He wanted to protest: the evidence, the expensive rug, but he said nothing.

'I opened drawers at random. Bank statements; old holiday bookings; credit-card records; letters; exhibition openings; all the usual stuff.

'In the middle drawer – isn't it supposed to be the bottom drawer in the films, Inspector? – there was a manilla envelope, underneath envelopes with the water rates and the gas bills in them, all labelled, just like John, very methodical. I'm surprised he hadn't written on the envelope: *Private: Love Letters*.

'The *bastard*. How could he do this to me? I'm dying of grief for him. I haven't slept since he died. I'm in agony for him. And all the time, he's had a secret affair.'

And then she did cry. Just let her head fall into her lap and sobbed and sobbed with all of her being.

Kavanagh moved uneasily on the sofa, leaned down towards her, put out a hand, but didn't touch her. He had never been able to cope with tears. Something to do with his mother, he imagined. He just had no idea what he was supposed to do. He knew from past experience that he wasn't expected to keep his distance, observe the situation clinically. Involvement was expected. Required, even. But the tears froze him. His hand hovered uncertainly above her shoulder as she wept.

'I'm sorry,' he said. 'Can I get you anything?'

She rocked her head from side to side. The worst was over; the tears were starting to abate, the breathing getting deeper. She eventually took a big, deep, nasal breath, drew herself up. She had a nice bosom. He found her extremely attractive, even with her mascara streaked and running down her cheeks. He passed her his clean handkerchief and she dabbed at her eyes with the white cotton square.

'May I?' she said, as she unfolded it and held it to her red nose.

'Please, of course,' he said graciously.

'I'm sorry,' she offered, unnecessarily.

'Please,' he said.

'Shall I go on?' she said.

'When you're ready,' he said.

'*Dear John; Darling John; John, sweetest love; Dearest John.* This is my *husband*, Inspector. The man I am grieving for. The man whose shoes I have just been pressing my fingers into to feel the shape of his foot.'

'I'm sorry,' said Kavanagh.

She looked up at him. There was a flash of recognition there. He was a man, as well. 'Yes, I'm sorry, too,' she said bitterly.

He felt a tinge of resentment. He didn't want to be tarred with the brush that was daubing Lacey. It seemed unfair. He'd had an affair or two during their long marriage, but so had Rachael. It was par for the course. He didn't know anyone who hadn't. But he was in a new situation; his present role was very different. He was victim; he was the aggrieved. He was suffering. It was too unfair that he should be miscast in this living-room production.

He knew all about lonely nights and terrible yearnings. He suspected betrayal now, too. His mind had started to run rampant with suspicions of deception and cheating. He was with her on this. They were together.

'May I see?' he asked, leaning forward and reaching for one of the letters.

'Of course,' she gestured with her hand. She sipped her Gordon's, stubbed out her cigarette and immediately lit another.

He glanced at the fulsome salutation, but before reading the contents of the letter, turned the page to see the signature. It ended with the words, 'All my love to you, Sarah.' He looked at a couple of the envelopes, held them up to read the South Wales postmarks.

He smiled. She caught the flicker on his face, looked up. 'Something amusing, Inspector?'

'Frank. Would you call me Frank, please? Can I take these?' he asked.

'Why not?' she said. 'Do you think they're important? Do you think dear Sarah' − she drawled the name out with contempt − 'has gone a bit loopy and come back and killed him after all these years? A woman spurned? It's a bit of a long shot, isn't it?'

'Yes, it is a long shot. But it's getting shorter.' He paused, looked at her carefully. 'How drunk are you?'

She was surprised by the candour of the inquiry; half drunk as she certainly was, she knew that it was too familiar, like someone asking you if you wore a bra or shaved your legs.

He didn't wait for an answer. 'Will you keep this to yourself?'

'Probably,' she said playfully. 'When you tell me what it is. I'm not insensible. I almost know what I'm doing.' She glanced up at him, and this time the recognition was nothing to do with his being simply male. It was entirely to do with himself, and herself.

'I actually like it when people say, "I've got something awful to tell you." There's that moment of suspense before you hear what it is. The "awful" is balanced by the excitement, like now, don't you think?'

Her knees were tucked under her. Her skirt had ridden

up her black tights. She was a bit drunk, but not crazy. The revelation about her husband's secret affair had devastated her, but it had also liberated her from her grief. These letters were the last thing she had wanted to find in the drawer of his desk amongst old Barclaycard statements. And yet, perversely, they had ameliorated her sadness.

'It's more than my job's worth,' he began, trying to communicate the seriousness of what he was telling her. 'But I want to tell you.'

'Yes?' she said.

'One of the other murder inquiries. One that I think might be linked with your . . .' He sought the word with difficulty, it no longer seemed entirely appropriate. '. . . with your husband's death . . .'

'Yes?' she said, intrigued.

'One of those other inquiries, possibly even two of them, may be related to someone with this initial,' he held one of the letters to her.

'I see,' she said, got uncertainly to her feet and went to the kitchen.

Kavanagh glanced from one letter to another, quickly read the contents. It was all personal, loving stuff: no politics or general knowledge, no sport. They were literate and loving, but the surprising thing was, they appeared to be one-way affairs.

But a note of need, then frustration, and eventually desperation crept into them. The recipient, Lacey, was either unable, or unwilling, to respond to these love letters.

They constantly asked for contact, a reciprocation of the feeling expressed in them, which evidently was never forthcoming. It occurred to the inspector that their author was either supremely confident, extremely callow, or just plain stupid.

Nowhere was there any inkling in the writer that the recipient might have, as Kavanagh felt certain must have

112

been the case, thought better of the relationship and was trying to withdraw from it.

Eventually the tone did change and manifest a little irritation and even irascibility as the author pleaded for a word: 'Literally one word, to show that those times mean and meant as much to you as they did to me. One word, on a card, in an envelope, anywhere, anyhow. Please.'

It was rather pathetic, thought Kavanagh.

Judith Lacey swayed back into the room, carrying a tray of coffee.

He took it from her. 'Do you know who this Sarah is?' he asked.

'Yes, I did. The absolute bitch. I'd like to pull her hair out and punch her in the face. I haven't felt like this since I was thirteen years old. I didn't know I could *have* these feelings. I'm sorry.'

'It's all right,' said Kavanagh. He knew about feelings of hatred. Even without the presence of another man to focus his resentment on, he had wished his ex-wife dead. Often. He knew all about the forces that drove those people in the papers who abducted wives, husbands, girl-friends, locked them in suburban sitting rooms and killed them all; or hired second-rate Liverpool criminals to murder them. She interrupted his downward-spiralling thoughts.

'John lodged with them in Cardiff when he did his MA there in the seventies.'

'And you met her?'

'A couple of times. I had the car up here. Sometimes, when he was coming home, I used to go down and pick him up. She was nice, or so I thought. A bit airy-fairy, younger than us, but very sweet. I had no idea just how sweet she was being to John. My God, the little bitch. I wonder if her husband knew, or even knows now. Perhaps I should get in touch with him?'

She was on a roll, unpacking her thoughts and fears in a stream-of-consciousness that Kavanagh recognized.

There was the initial shock of revelation, but soon she would be falling headlong into the chasm of grief where there would be few jokes and little comfort and much pain.

She picked up her thread of the past again. 'Her husband was older than her, they had a little girl, just a toddler. They seemed a nice couple. John liked them straight-away.'

'And you had no idea?'

'Knock me over with a feather. I'm amazed. Do you know what I don't understand? When did all this happen? You know, John was working hard for his MA; her husband was doing teacher training after his degree, and she was presumably looking after their child. When did they . . . you know . . . when did they find the time, the oppor-tunity?'

'I think her husband went away. There was some involvement with someone else, a friend of her husband's. The husband went away for a few days so that she and this bloke could . . . "sort it out". I suppose your . . . hus-band and she might have . . . you know.'

'Who *is* this woman for Christ's sake? She's having an affair with someone, her husband goes away, and then she fits in a little number on the side with my husband the lodger at the same time? My God, who the hell is this woman?'

'I don't know. But I'm sure I'll be seeing her soon.'

'When you said the other inquiries might be linked, how many more are there?'

'Not a word. All right? I know all this is terrible and a shock for you, but really, I'd lose my job.' He didn't wait for her affirmation, but he knew he could trust her.

'There have been three deaths recently: your husband; the man I've just mentioned, and with whom she had an affair, and another man, whom we think she met much more recently, in the eighties, when she was at Open University summer school . . .'

114

'What was she doing, Greek Tragedy?'

He smiled. 'Three relationships, all the men and one of their wives now dead, and killed in violent circumstances.'

'But why would she do this? Why is she killing these men that she's had relationships with? Surely it's *me*, and the other women, who should be killing *her*, or our own husbands.'

'I've no idea. I agree it makes no sense. None at all.'

'And why now? After all this time? Why is she doing it now?'

'I really don't know. It's a mystery, but we're looking for her. We'll find her and find out, of that I'm sure.'

She sipped her coffee; there was a little self-consciousness between them. She had spent her initial salvo. It was just the two of them now.

She placed her cup on the saucer and glanced up at him. There was a look between them that said, 'Well, what do you think?'

There was fellow feeling. A common agenda. Kavanagh's wife had left him; Judith Lacey's husband had been killed, but had cheated her, taken his sordid secret to the grave and left her punching air. There was a ridiculous, gung-ho, 'Well, why not us, too?' atmosphere between them.

She was fairly drunk; he liked her. But he knew that soon she would be playing the long game, feeling deep pain, not just the almost exciting, drunken miasma of emotion that accompanied the impact of discovery. Knowing this, he knew that he should not seek to take advantage of her.

'Would you like me to stay the night?'

She looked up. Her eyes said, 'Yes,' she would do it, but also acknowledged the lack of conviction in his request.

He responded instantly to her ambivalence, decided, on this occasion at least, to play for the draw, end with a handshake and a 'well played'. 'I don't mean *with* you. I mean here, on the sofa. Just so there's someone around?'

She smiled. They were both well ahead of the game. 'It's a nice thought,' she said, 'but I'll be all right, really.'

'Are you sure?' he said, a little regretfully, not sure that he couldn't simply chip a winner into the top corner by stealth alone. It might, after all, be the right thing for them both. Who knows?

'Perhaps another time?' she said.

16

Sarah Clarke was living in north London. She had changed her name by deed poll, in 1991. Kavanagh's need to speak to her had become pressing: while he had been sitting with Judith Lacey the previous evening, the Bursar's office of the Open University in Milton Keynes had telephoned DCs Denny and Reeder with the names of female students whose initials were SC, and who had been at Keele in the summer of 1985.

There were three: Sonia Coultard; Sally Cummings and, the only one of the three to have been there during the same week as Terry Sugar, Sarah Clarke.

Presley picked up his boss at his house in Erdington and drove them into Birmingham city centre. At the traffic lights on Colmore Row, Kavanagh watched as a pretty shop girl kissed her boyfriend goodbye for the day.

As the inspector watched the youngsters, Presley glanced at his boss. The man had changed: something had left him.

'Did you ever see *The Accidental Tourist*?' said Kavanagh.

Presley tapped the accelerator for his routine grid start, even though they had half an hour before the train's departure.

'No. Don't think so,' he said, concentrating on the cars on either side of him. And then, judging that he still had a second to proffer a modicum of response, 'Why?'

'William Hurt says, "It's not how much you love someone, but what matters is who you are when you're with them." Something like that, anyway.'

The lights went to amber and Presley left the cars on either side of him standing. 'Yes?' he said.

'It's a good film,' said Kavanagh, pressed back into the passenger seat. 'You'd love it!'

Presley swung the car round the concrete pillars and tight bends of the multi-storey car park on Hill Street. Before he locked the Granada, he reached into the driver's side-door pocket, pulled out a pair of stained Y-front underpants and draped them on his seat.

'Do you *have* to do that?' said Kavanagh.

'Never fails,' said Presley, jauntily.

They took the 8.15 inter-city out of New Street. Presley would have driven. Hurtled down the M1, inviolable in their official car, the three-litre Ford passing everything in sight.

But, given the choice, Kavanagh always travelled by train. He liked them: their indomitability, their power, their huge, mechanical strength.

Off it went, fixed on its silver tracks, out past the British Small Arms factory; past the Dogs' Home with its fascia of jolly puppies; past the grey, deserted go-cart track, Birmingham City's football ground in the distance. And eventually, gathering speed, through the allotments and extensions, greenhouses, satellite dishes and back gardens of south Birmingham.

In only ten minutes, the bramble, elder and discarded mattresses of the suburbs had given way to birch and ash and pollarded willow, grubby sheep and ploughed fields.

Yes, thought Kavanagh, slumped in his seat by the window, he certainly preferred this to Presley's flying down the motorway at a hundred miles an hour.

Travel by train was, for Kavanagh, inexorably bound up with childhood: the memory of distant summer holidays to Lytham St Anne's, the rail journey as much a prerequisite of the August excursion as was the four-storey guesthouse, set one street back from the sedate promenade and its expensive hotels.

The images crowded his vision: he and his brother in a prepubescent joy of bucket and spade, sand castles, paper flags on balsa sticks, fishing nets and model boats with their beautiful, deep-varnished hulls on the pond that was a summer's evening ocean, a mere nine inches deep.

By fourteen, the unselfconscious child had metamorphosed into a surly adolescent: James Dean on Lytham's promenade, a scowling youth in jeans and black linen, zippered jerkin determinedly leaning away from the little family group as they were snapped en route to the beach.

His sister at fifteen, pirouetting on the sand, glimpses of her secrets as she changed into her swimming costume, wrapped only in a beach towel. The boys from Lancashire and Scotland, like flies around her throughout the day, swatted away by their vigilant mother.

The flat, grey sea; the unrelenting August heat; children's voices all around; face down, an intermittent erection in the sand, sweat trickling through dark eyebrows.

Cliff Richard's 'Living Doll'; long afternoons on the beach; Lyon's Maid strawberry Mivvies for the children; Wall's ice-creams for the grown-ups, his mother drawing her tongue up between the wafer biscuits, leaning forward to catch the melting stuff; his father asleep in his deck chair beneath an immaculately constructed newspaper hat.

The interminable, silent ritual of the three-course evening meal, followed, an agony of waiting later, by a walk along the dusky front beneath the softly glowing, coloured lamps.

And now, in his mid-forties, this train, *any* train, could readily evoke the piquant memory of those times.

Kavanagh observed in the reflection of the glass the couple sitting opposite him. He had become inordinately, mawk-

119

ishly interested in relationships. The insipid misogyny that had crept, unnoticed, into his very being, like ink into blotting paper, had become recently a deeper-hued misanthropy. Men, in particular, were a despicable species: their oppression and bullying born of nothing but fear and weakness.

Kavanagh was full of self-loathing. The age-old conundrum, the one whose truth he had recognized since he was a twitchy adolescent, the quintessential Groucho Marx line: *I wouldn't want to belong to any club that would accept me as a member*, had become his mantra.

I covet her; she accepts me; I do not love myself; *ergo*: if she loves me, she cannot be worthy of my love. *I wouldn't want to belong to any club that would accept me as a member*. Round and round. A rodent on a wheel.

It had started with Sandra Dolan, an unimaginable prize. Fifteen, dark eyes, deep, mysterious womanhood. He had caught his own father looking at her as a man looks at a woman.

Bosomy, sexual, frightening, exciting; they had done it one half-term afternoon in the bedroom he shared with his brother, the suburban house deserted.

She had known what to do, which garments to remove, which to leave on – 'Your mother might come back' – and he had come in a flash of ecstatic, wild excitement.

He didn't call for her again. He took the long way round to the bus to avoid her house. He didn't want her. Not at all. *Any club . . .*

She took up with Alan Hammond from the council estate, a dangerous, unpredictable boy. Young Kavanagh looked longingly at her. Wrote letters and poems that were never sent, peered at her from behind the bedroom curtains as she passed.

And so it went on. Down all the years, repeatedly: the apparently unattainable, attained. And then the inexorable process of rejection. Rachael had been so loving, so long-suffering, so *good* really, that it had taken him nearly twenty years to prise her love away and force her rejection of him.

But eventually, the scouring drip of his own self-loathing had worn her spirit away. He had managed it. He had estranged her so thoroughly, so completely, that she had finally left him. He was, once more, alone and cold.

And although it hurt, especially at that darkest hour, just before dawn, he knew, even then, that this *was* his rightful place, this *was* where he belonged. *Any club* . . .

The man opposite droned on, talking figures and budgets and costs. His plain, female colleague listened intently.

Kavanagh hated this man with a ferocious contempt: his facial hair, his bad suit and ill-chosen tie; his noisy yawn when he eschewed putting his hand to his mouth. 'Look, I hate her,' said his every gesture. 'I cover her with my stomach's bad breath.'

Later, he flitted in and out of articles in the newspaper. She filled in the *Daily Telegraph* crossword.

The inspector knew that she was brighter than her colleague. He was sure that she read proper novels, listened to *From Our Own Correspondent* on Radio Four, watched current affairs on TV.

Outside Birmingham's International station, she took her jacket, and he gathered his pens and photocopied figures and newspaper into a shiny, black, FisherPrice briefcase, concealing them from the world behind an array of combination locks and brass hinges.

Presley went to the buffet car for coffee.

The train passed a siding with a dozen, summer-blue painted trucks in it, weeds growing high up their sides.

Did someone in British Rail *know* about these wagons, their flaps down, their cargo long-since disembarked? They looked as if they had been there for years.

And since when had British Rail painted its freight trucks blue? They were pretty, like you might see on a clockwork model railway. But this was a siding some-where between Coventry and somewhere else.

Was someone in an office, somewhere, aware of these twelve blue wagons, languishing in the sun, like old pit ponies taken up out of the dark and left quietly to pasture?

The train thundered through cavernous, open-to-the-sky Rugby without stopping. Presley brought the coffee. Kavanagh wondered about the trucks. He thought about Rachael. He tried again to think about the trucks.

Two nights ago, he had finally given in. At three in the morning, well over the limit, he had driven his old Citroën DS the three or four miles to her flat on the other side of the city.

He had sat outside for an hour, smoking and watching the still room above the empty street. When his eyes adjusted to the darkness of the scene, he began to make out the shapes on the windowsill.

There was a soft light filtering through from the landing into the sitting-room. Perhaps she *was* alone, his convic-tion that she was with someone else no more than a fig-ment of three a.m. paranoia.

She had always slept with the light on outside their bedroom door if she was alone.

On the windowsill was a plant, a camellia, perhaps, something late in bloom and, further along, a vase full of big overstated flowers, perhaps gladioli or African lilies.

He'd never known her buy African lilies before. Perhaps they were the gift of someone. If someone was buying her flowers, were they with her now? Were they making love, at this moment, while he sat outside, ridiculous, looking up at the window from his pale grey Citroën with its beautiful maroon roof?

The sweat of anguish poured from him. Was she holding someone in her arms, calling him into her as they made love?

Everything was soft and beautiful and quiet there. It

was so simple, so delightful. And he was outside of it.

Should he go and ring the bell? Wake her up and beg her to come back? And if there was someone there, what then? He would kill him. Of that, there was simply no doubt. At the door, half dressed; in her room, naked. In the bathroom, washing her from himself. He would kill him.

This was the woman he had learned to overlook, who had done everything for him, and whom he had reduced to nothing. She was now giving herself to someone else. He knew he had to drive away. If the figure of a man cast a shadow across the yellow lamplight as he walked to the bathroom, or went for a cigarette, he would go up there and kill him. And her, and then himself.

Fight or flight? He drove away, flew through the empty Birmingham streets in his loping Citroën, drank half a bottle of Scotch in huge glugs that would not still his thoughts or anaesthetize his brain into oblivion.

Eventually, collapsed on the sofa, haunted by thoughts of gaudy flowers on a windowsill, garish lilies, risible pink gladioli, he imagined again that he was holding her, only to wake, cold and bitter, deeply sad and entirely alone.

The next day, wretched, sleepless, hung over, while the rest of the team went to the local pub for their customary pie and two pints, he had returned.

He parked around the corner and walked down an alley to the rear of her flat, drawn inexorably to the scene of her life.

He lifted the Suffolk latch on the white, wooden gate, peered in at the little patch of garden.

He was distraught to see the results of her labour. Even now, in early November, it was lovely.

There was a flower border on either side of the gravel path with the frosted remains of self-seeded, translucent nasturtiums winding through the random terracotta pots that were dotted there.

She had bought lots of winter-flowering pansies, their

garish colours of yellow and black and blue belying their wavering frailty. And against the red-brick wall there were big clumps of montbretia, planted long ago by some former tenant, and still revealing remnants of their orange flowers. All of her favourite things.

He knew that beneath the dark loam would be tulip bulbs, streaked, papery carapaces of jaunty daffodils and, even as he stood there, shivering at his exclusion, anemone corms, shouldering themselves out of their inauspicious woody husks.

He stood at the gate of the empty, quiet garden. He was the face at the window, the spectre: unable to break free, to go on, to start afresh, to make the new life.

He'd known men like this before, but he hadn't recognized their plight. Now, to his chagrin, he realized that he'd felt nothing but a kind of resentful contempt for them, as if, without his knowing exactly why, they deserved their fate.

Were all women like this? Did they all cope so much better than men with almost everything? They had more fortitude, more resolve, more inner strength, he'd always known that. It was nothing to do with all that endlessly repeated Thatcher nonsense. Gender was patently *not* the point with Margaret Thatcher. She was as rare and strange, unique really, as any of those curiosities of history: Boadicea or Napoleon or Cleopatra.

Kavanagh meant ordinary women, everyday women. The women in the pub and on the train and in the office or playing darts. Yes, of course they couldn't arm wrestle or kick a ball so far, but the stuff that mattered, really mattered, this, life, they could certainly manage that better; infinitely better.

No wonder they loathed men. No wonder they were doing without Frank Kavanagh and his ilk.

He sat in the deep seat of the car, its leather worn and scuffed into something that was his shape and person, started the engine and pushed the column-change up into first. The car rose magically those few French inches, inches that distinguished it from every other car, and its makers from every other nation.

The shipping forecast was just beginning on Radio Four. These things: the Citroën DS that he had driven for ten years and loved; the music that introduced *Desert Island Discs*; the comfort of Bailey and Rockall, Fair Isle and Mallinhead; the words that briskly issued in another day: 'And now, the weather forecast for the United Kingdom, until dawn tomorrow'; he clung to the certainty of these things, flotsam that might yet, even in this bilious sea of change, see him safely to the shore.

It was over. That glimpse of her life through the white, wooden gate set in the red-brick wall was more eloquent than any number of words.

Until that moment, he had secretly fed his life with notions of a reconciliation.

On that Tuesday lunch time, driving through the Stratford Road traffic, the sea fog off Southeast Iceland 'gathering slowly', he knew that their life together was finally over. It granted him a kind of peace, like the amputation of a painful limb, before its final, irredeemable loss is understood.

Kavanagh and Presley wandered through the marble concourse and down to the subterranean taxi rank.

The driver of their black cab didn't acknowledge in any way Presley's instruction to take them to Brecknock Road, just pushed up the window, slotted the excess fare onto the meter, and inched forward into the relentless flow of traffic on bleak Cardington Street.

Kavanagh could drive all right, but in London the cars and cabs beavered and nosed and eased into impossible places, manoeuvred through logic-defying spaces.

Another six inches, another six inches, the oncoming drivers holding their nerve against the bull-nosed throbbing diesel until there was nowhere else for it to go but out, out into the ever-moving stream.

There was something about Londoners' savoir-faire, a resignation which amounted almost to stoicism, and which intrigued Kavanagh. He suspected that there might have been a covert infiltration of the capital's entire population, like that in the *Invasion of the Bodysnatchers* or *The Stepford Wives*. The people were, certainly, unmistakably, different.

There was a resignation, an acceptance of their city falling apart. It was there from early morning, with the young people in blankets and cardboard boxes in their doorways, one hand extended: 'Can you spare any change, please? Can you spare some change?'

And it was there in the parked cars with their smashed quarter-lights, black plastic crudely taped and flapping in the breeze; in the graffiti that adorned the boarded-up churches and every bus stop and wall; it was there in the huge fire engines, sirens blaring, as they swung heavy around corners and through the parting traffic; and it was there as no one even looked up at the beautiful, big, silver jets droning by above their heads, throttling back as they dropped through the mackerel skies down to Gatwick and Heathrow.

Has earth anything to show more fair?

Occasionally, that resignation was a quiet and charming thing, and even the battle-hardened taxi driver played a strange, forgiving part as he let a scruffy minicab or a student's battered Fiat into the traffic of Holloway Road.

More usually, though, battle *was* joined, but it was with the phut of a buried grenade, the shrapnel zing ameliorated by the sand of familiarity. These people had seen it all before, saw it every day. Every third person on the street was mad or bad or violent or drunk.

It frightened Kavanagh: in a place like this, if you fell down in Charing Cross or King's Cross, you would certainly lie there, unattended and unhelped.

126

Everyone feared the danger of strangers, even fallen strangers, with their hypodermics and Carlsbergs and dogs and vomit. And in this city, *everyone* was a stranger.

'Seven pounds,' said the cabbie, without turning round. Presley paid him through the half-open window.

The two policemen stood on the Brecknock Road pavement and looked up at Sarah Clarke's flat.

17

Sarah Clarke, circa 1991, had become Sarah Hardy.

She was tall, slim and attractive. Her hair was streaked with fine, long grey hairs amidst the blonde. She was forty-two, Kavanagh knew, but looked five years younger.

She led the two policemen up the stairs and into the spacious front room above the furniture shop that looked down on bustling Brecknock Road in Camden.

He'd told her on the phone that it was about an old acquaintance. Any one from three. He'd chosen Sugar because he was the most recent. A mere eight years ago. If the stories panned out, her relationships with Lacey and Curtiss went back nearly two decades.

She had been intrigued. But he had avoided giving her the whole story, and time to reflect and, possibly, clam up.

You never knew how people would react. And it was in seeing their reaction, first time, as the story came out, that you learned about them.

She made them tea and offered her packet of Benson and Hedges with a slightly shaking hand.

'Thank you, Ms . . .' said Kavanagh. 'It's Ms Hardy now, not Clarke. Is that right?'

'Yes. I changed my name a couple of years ago, after my marriage ended.'

'I see,' he said. 'As I said on the phone, it's just a few questions, about Terry Sugar.'

'Yes?' she said.

He glanced around the room. 'You said to me that you have a "friend". Does he live here too?'

'Some of the time. I rent the flat and Peter rents the shop downstairs,' she said. 'He stays over sometimes. But he has a place of his own, too.'

'What does he do?' asked Presley.

'He restores furniture; strips pine, that kind of thing,' she said; and then, apparently keen to get on, 'Why are you here?' she asked directly.

'We need to fill out the picture, about what I mentioned on the phone. I'll explain as we go along,' said Kavanagh, appearing to trade off, say something, in fact giving nothing. 'Do you work at the moment? Do you have a job?'

'I work in an old people's home. I'm a supervisor there.'

'I see. And how long have you lived here?'

'About two years. Since my marriage broke up. Look, before you ask *me* any more questions, would you tell me about Terry. Is he in trouble?'

Kavanagh looked at Presley. It was a reasonable question. But they didn't want to reveal that they knew about her likely relationship with him at Open University. It was important that they should see what she would give them, volunteer unasked.

Kavanagh said, appearing to answer her, 'Do you know his background?'

'A bit,' she said guardedly. 'I didn't know him well. We were close for a short time. How do you know that I knew him?'

'From . . . documents,' said Kavanagh evasively. 'Tell us about your relationship with him.'

'Why?' she said, this time curt. 'I'm not sure I *want* to tell you. It's personal.'

'It is important,' said Kavanagh, conciliatory.

'Why?' she insisted.

He answered her with a question: 'Do you ever see *Crimewatch*, Ms Hardy?'

'No. Why?'

'Terry Sugar was featured on the programme recently. I'm afraid he's dead.' He watched for the Polaroid reaction of the woman in front of him and continued, 'He was killed. Some weeks ago now.'

She was moved by the news, but certainly not shocked.

If she knew about his heroin habit, and with both his inner arms like perished cycle tubes, and veins that stood a quarter of an inch up from the flesh, it would be difficult to avoid it, she might reasonably assume that his death was drug related.

'You don't seem very surprised, Ms Hardy?'

'I know he had some drug problems. And anyway, when a policeman from Birmingham says he's tracked you down through Inland Revenue and tells you he's coming to London to "ask you a few questions about an old friend", I suppose you know it's not a parking offence he's looking into.'

'Yes, you're right, of course. And we need very badly to fill in some of the gaps in his life; his relationships. It's where you come in.'

She nodded agreement. She was going to play.

'We met at summer school a few years ago. It was 1985, I think. I'd have to check.' (It *was* '85, Kavanagh felt like saying; July '85.) 'We . . . had an affair.' She rolled her cigarette ash around the ashtray.

'And?' said Presley, too quickly.

'And what?' she said, challenging, feeling herself being judged by two men who had nothing to do with her, and no right to be asking her about her personal life.

'Was that it?' said Kavanagh, attempting to mollify.

'Yes. More or less. We spoke on the phone. But we didn't meet again. It just fizzled out.'

'You were married at that time?'

'Yes. What is this? The Vatican Council? It's a knocking shop,' she said with fierce sarcasm. 'Everybody knows that.' She looked at Presley, dared him to contradict her, her big brown eyes facing him out.

'People go there for a good time. OK, there's a few anoraks and winceyette pyjamas, a few eager beavers going to lectures and back to their rooms to study, but mostly, for the staff *and* the students, it's just an opportunity to . . . to get together.'

Both men knew plenty of coppers who'd done OU courses, summer school, the whole bit. Yes, it helped your career to have a degree in law or psychology or sociology, and yes, they both knew guys who, one way or another, were now divorced. (One sergeant's wife had even cited the OU as the correspondent in her divorce proceedings.) But whether the kind of people who did OU stuff were susceptible to marital breakdown, or whether the Open University was *responsible* for those divorces, neither man knew.

She carried on, 'It's no secret. It's an auction. You take your pick. Men and women. Here today, gone home to the wife and kids and washing-up or washing the car tomorrow.

'Everyone's been filled up with this liberal education for twelve months, struggling with assignments and tutorials and essays and early-morning and late-night TV. All that poetry and history and politics, and then there's this. They're similar people, have the same hunger, they know what you've been through, there's lots to talk about, to share. And it's the end.'

'The end?' said Presley.

'The end of term,' she said, smiling. 'School's out.'

Kavanagh was quite moved. It might, as she had gracelessly said, be a 'knocking shop' (a crude and distasteful phrase, wholly out of character with her, he thought) but she certainly made a case, in spite of herself really, for its educational value.

But he was less interested in the educational benefits of Jennie Lee's landmark creation than in the specifics of Sarah Hardy and Terry Sugar's affair.

'Did your husband know about your . . . relationship?'

'Not at the time, no.' And then, after a pause, 'I think he suspected something. People do know, I think, don't they?' she said, looking from Kavanagh to Presley and back again.

'Yes, I think people know,' said Kavanagh.

'I did tell him. But it was much later.'

'And what happened next?' prompted Presley, taking his more conciliatory tone from his boss.

'With Terry? It was impossible: my trying to get out of the house; his phoning me at a call box . . .'

'You were living in Shrewsbury then?' said Kavanagh, ever methodical, ever keen to slot the events and places neatly where they belonged.

'Yes. Jeff was teaching at a school there. Anyway, Terry, I don't think his heart was in it. I thought I was in love. I always do.' She smiled fleetingly. 'Or maybe I just have to: convince myself I'm in love so it doesn't seem like some cheap little affair.

'I think Terry *was* fond of me. Well, I know he was, but I don't think he was ready to leave home, give up his pitch on the High Street, leave his wife, the whole business. He was settled, and he'd got his habit, which softened most of the knocks he had to take.'

There was a pause. She became reflective. The policemen were prudently silent.

'He was a nice man. He'd got some problems, of course. But he was nice. I liked him a lot. Did he get some bad stuff?'

'He was killed.'

'Yes,' she said. 'But was it bad stuff?'

'No. He was killed deliberately. In his car. He was gassed to death. And his wife.'

'My God! He was murdered?'

'Yes, I'm afraid so.'

'I just . . . I just assumed it was bad stuff, cut with something, you know. Or some nasty deal. This is awful.'

'It could have been drug related,' said Presley.

132

'Yes, it might have been,' continued Kavanagh. 'We've got to keep an open mind. But there are other connections, things that need to be tied up. There's a possible link, too much for coincidence . . .'

'With what?' she asked guilelessly.

'Possibly with you,' said Kavanagh.

'With me?' she said, actually pointing the long fingers of her left hand at her chest.

'Did you have other affairs?' asked the inspector.

'Why?'

'I have to ask you these things, believe me.'

'Why do you?' she said.

'Please, Ms Hardy, it's very important. People have been murdered. Other lives might be at risk.'

'I don't understand.'

'Did you have another affair? More than one?'

'No.'

'Are you sure?'

'Am I sure?' she said bitingly. 'Don't you mean: "Are you telling the truth?" I *know* whether I have affairs or not.'

'What about further back in the past?'

'What about it?'

'Did you have any . . . extramarital relationships then?'

'Yes. Did *you*?'

'Ms Hardy,' said Kavanagh with a mock weariness, 'this is serious. Very serious. We're not playing. Whoever murdered Terry Sugar and his wife may have killed other people you knew. There seems to be a link.'

She was agitated, frightened: didn't know whether to believe them or not. Was this just the way they did things, by frightening people?

'Who that I "knew" has been killed?'

'Did you have any other relationships during your marriage?'

'Why?'

He wouldn't let go. 'Please, Ms Hardy, answer my questions first. Tell us about your relationships, no matter how long ago. Then I'll tell you what I know. I promise.'

'It's all so distant, like another life really. We married young. I was barely twenty. And I was having a baby.

'He was older than me, three or four years older. It was an unequal relationship from the start. He made all the decisions. It couldn't be any other way. He was the one with the information. I think he loved me for my youth; I *was* pretty. But he always made me feel insignificant and silly. I had to survive, stay alive somehow.' She paused, sucked on her cigarette, looked from Kavanagh to Presley and back again.

'So, you had an affair?' said Kavanagh sympathetically, encouraging her to start again.

'Yes. It wasn't a conscious fighting back. But I was disappearing, and it was my only way of asserting myself, I suppose. I didn't work it out or anything.'

'Who was it?' said Presley.

'Do I have to?' she said, looking at Kavanagh.

'Please,' said the inspector gently.

'It was a friend of his. A man called Adam. Adam Curtiss.'

'Go on,' said Kavanagh.

'Jeff wasn't blameless, you know,' she said defensively. '*He* had affairs too.'

'Yes. But for now, just tell us about yourself. Please, carry on.'

'We were living in Cardiff. Jeff was finishing his course. There was someone living with us, a lodger. They were very different times. We were young, things were different in every way. We were having a bad time. I had an affair with Jeff's friend, Adam. I ran away to London to be with him. Jeff came and took me back.

'It was all awful. Then Jeff went away to let me sort things out. Left me at home with Briony, our daughter.

'Adam came to see me and stayed a couple of days. But

134

it didn't work out. How could it? And he went back to London.

'It was then I had a brief fling with the man who was living with us, a man called John, John Lacey. I know it sounds awful, and in a way it was, but I was lost, unhappy with Jeff, and struggling to find a way out. It was insane really, the whole thing.'

'And your husband?' said Kavanagh quietly. 'He knew about this?'

'He knew about Adam. I told him about John much later, when things were better between us, and I wanted him to know everything, so we could start fresh.'

'How did he take it?' said Presley.

'Badly.'

'How badly?'

'He was very upset. Very hurt.'

'And?'

She sighed. 'And it passed. And we got on and tried to put things back together.'

'Go on,' urged Kavanagh.

'Things were all right for a while. For several years. Not brilliant, but better. Best we'd ever been. He could still bruise me with a word. But we were older.

'I'd grown up and I'd learned how to handle him: and he'd learned to be better to me. He knew I could hurt him, too. I was working. Briony was growing up. We were getting along.'

'Yes?' said Kavanagh. There was no point in interrupting. This was her story. He let her run with it.

'Everyone else we knew had a degree, they were all "educated". My father was in the army. I had been to five schools in eleven years when I was a child.

'So I enrolled for the Open University; got up early, watched the morning BBC2 broadcasts and got to quite like the regime of tea and my notepad and books spread about me, the men in flared trousers talking about architecture and the growth of literacy.

135

'I met Terry at summer school. He hadn't been out of prison long, and there he was, with all these housewives and teachers, tattoos on both his forearms, short hair, and a heroin habit.

'But he was sharp. Bright but vulnerable. Worse off than me, even. I liked him; there didn't seem any point in not going with him. I didn't have enough to make me not want to. Not really.

'I gave myself to him. I think he was surprised. He didn't even have to ask.

'Afterwards, we spoke on the phone, but it just faded away, shrivelled up from lack of contact. Jeff and I slipped back into our routine. And there we stayed, another few years.

'Briony had grown up. She was twenty, she had left home, was at university in Aberystwyth.'

She sighed very deeply.

'I wanted us to have a baby. I needed Jeff to show me that he loved me. I think that's all that I had ever needed from him. That's why I had kept on hurting him.

'But he didn't want one. He put up all the practical reasons for our not having one. Good, sound, sensible reasons why we shouldn't do it. He wanted to give up his job teaching. Wanted early retirement. Was looking for less responsibility, not more. He was trying to get his book written.'

'He was writing a book?' asked Kavanagh.

'Yes, an academic book. A critical work on Gerard Manley Hopkins.'

'And did he?' said Kavanagh, intrigued. 'Did he finish it?'

'Yes, eventually, he did. He kept at it. It was his "baby". Do you see?' she said, smiling slightly, without joy. 'And I wanted mine.

'He said the only way he'd be a father again would be if his book was published. He quoted all that Cyril Connolly nonsense about creativity going out of the window as soon as there's a pram in the hall.'

'And was it?' asked Kavanagh.

'No. No, it wasn't. Not in the end. But it looked as if it was going to be.

'He finished it, and sent it out, again, and again, and again. And every time, it just kept coming back.

'At first, it was a real body blow. But after the first two or three times, he became very stoical, and just mailed it out again.

'One day, instead of his book coming back, a letter came. It was a small academic publisher who said yes.'

'They took it?' said Kavanagh, really quite excited by the story.

'Yes. They accepted it. No advance, just royalties on sales. It was the best day of his life, he said.

'I came off the pill. It was what we had said. He'd agreed: if his book was taken, we could have our baby.

'Months went by: letters, phone calls, but no book. Always some reason for the delay: the estate, copyright, the man's partner out of the country, but Jeff knew things weren't right.

'And then, one day, he telephoned the man's number, a little office somewhere in Herefordshire, and there was no reply.

'He'd gone bust. Jeff's book wasn't going to get printed.

'The same week, I found out that I was pregnant. His baby dying, mine trying to be born.

'I nurtured my secret, a warm glow of a lovely secret. Not the wrong kind of deceit that we had known all too much of during our marriage, but a secret wish that was mine and that we had agreed to.'

She stopped speaking, took shallow breaths, was very close to tears.

'Please, go on,' he said gently.

'The next morning, I took him a cup of coffee. I put the

coffee cup down on the chair beside the bed next to the radio alarm.

'He opened his eyes and said, "What's the matter?"

'I held up the little tube that had gone pink. "I'm pregnant," I said.

'"Oh, no!" he said. "Oh no!" and held me to him.

'I went to see my doctor that evening. He confirmed that I was pregnant.

'I told him that Jeff wasn't sure about us having another baby. He said that by the time he was bouncing the little baby on his knee, he wouldn't have any reservations.

'But the doctor was wrong. Jeff said that he *really* didn't want another baby. He was forty-four, he kept saying.

'"You said if your book was taken we could have a baby. You said it. You *said* it. And I held on to that belief."'

'"I know I said it, but the book *isn't* being published. They've gone out of business."'

'"But you said . . ."'

'"I know what I said. And I shouldn't have done."

'I told him that I couldn't have a termination. There was a life inside me; I couldn't do it.'

'"We had our child,"' he said. "We could have been happy then . . ."'

She looked from one policeman to the other, hopelessly, pleading. 'I was being punished for our past. I wanted us to be happy. It was so easy, couldn't he see? Just let's do this wonderful thing.

'But *I* had been to blame for the bad part of our marriage, and now he was going to punish me for it by not having a baby with me.

'My best friend took me to the hospital. I was in a ward with six other women. I dozed and cried into my pillow.

'They gave me my premed, and took me down just before eleven o'clock. That's all I remember.

'When I woke up it was about two o'clock, and all of the other ladies were lying in their beds with drips and tubes.

'I looked at them but kept my head on the pillow and then closed my eyes and went back into a sort of sleep.

'They brought me some tea and asked me how I was and helped me sit up. I kept myself inside and smiled and said thank you and drank the milky tea.

'At five, Jeff came. He had flowers and a card.

'I said I was all right, but I said I didn't want to talk about things right now.

'We drove home slowly.

'On the Monday, I went back to work, and in the evening Jeff asked me if it was all right if he went out for a drink. He said he wouldn't mind if I didn't want him to go. He would quite understand.

'I said I didn't mind.'

She started to cry.

'Both our babies died. And our hopeless marriage, too. "Why must disappointment all I endeavour end . . ."'

'Sorry?' said Kavanagh.

'It's Hopkins. Gerard Manley Hopkins. He always used to say it when his book was rejected: ". . . and not breed one work that wakes." Very appropriate,' she murmured.

'I wanted to hurt him. I wanted to hurt him as much as he had hurt me.

'I knew the one thing that *would* destroy him . . . but I couldn't do it.

'I wanted to. But I couldn't.

'I told him, instead, about my affair with Terry all those years ago, at summer school.

'He asked me things. Asked me what we had *done*. And I told him. I told him everything.

'He shouldn't have made me do that thing. It was our baby. It was wrong. And *I* have to live with that.

'I'm not really an unfaithful woman. I know it sounds silly. But I'm not. Not deep down. I just needed to be loved.'

There was a long silence, with only the rumble and whine of the constant traffic in the street below.

Eventually, Kavanagh said quietly, 'What was the thing you were going to tell him, Ms Hardy? That would have destroyed him?'

'I can't tell you. I've never told anyone. I never will.'

'Whatever it is, are you sure he hasn't found out?' asked the inspector.

'No, he doesn't know.'

'And you won't tell me, in confidence?'

'No,' she said quietly, but resolutely. 'No.'

'I see.' Kavanagh drew a deep breath. 'Where is he now, Ms Hardy? Do you know?'

'He went away. He gave up teaching; well, they gave him up really, he had a sort of breakdown. He went to live in Cheshire, and then I think he went abroad. Left me to sell the house, which I did, and Peter and I moved away, came down here.'

'And your ex-husband? Is he still in touch?'

'No. We made all the financial arrangements through our solicitors, but there was no personal contact. At first he sent a few crazy letters, almost deranged really: grief, regret, anger, jealousy. Peter said I shouldn't read them. After a while I didn't. They were too upsetting.

'And then we moved and I changed my name. I don't think he knows where I am. I hope not.'

She became reflective again, almost ignored Kavanagh and Presley's presence. 'It's funny, isn't it, the person you have everything with, the person you would do anything with and for, they eventually become the person you avoid most completely, even hide from. I've never been able to get over that.

'Briony used to write to him, but I think even that's stopped now. She's in Wales, in Machynlleth. As part of her degree course.

'I've told her not to tell him where we are. I was afraid of him, to be honest. I think he was capable of anything.'

18

An hour later, she escorted them to the top of the steep stairs. They had told her the little that she needed to know about the violent deaths of her former lovers, Adam Curtiss and John Lacey.

At the street door, Kavanagh turned and said to her, 'We'll just have a word with your friend downstairs. Is he in the shop?'

'Yes, I think so. Why?' she said.

'Just a precaution,' said Kavanagh. 'Keep an eye out for anything unusual, Ms Hardy. I'll have one of the local CID watch the place, too. And let me know if you hear anything at all from your ex-husband.

'When we've finished in London, probably tomorrow, we'll go up and see your daughter, just in case he's been in touch with her.'

'You think he might come here?' she said, concerned.

'I don't know. The deaths are too much for coincidence. And you are the link. But it doesn't make sense: all this time passed.' He paused and smiled up at her. '*You* haven't been killing people, have you?'

She smiled at his bad-taste joke. 'No, I haven't killed anyone.'

'Oh, yes, Ms Hardy, one thing . . .'

'Yes?'

'Your ex-husband?'

'Yes?'

'What size shoes did he wear?'

'Are you serious?'

'Yes. What size, please?'

'Ten; ten and a half, I think. Why?'

'It's nothing. Just a thought. Thank you. Goodbye.'

Next door, in the pine shop, they introduced themselves to the man in Levis and Timberland boots, told him they were concerned about Sarah Hardy's former husband, thought he might be able to help them with their inquiries.

Peter Burchell was Scots, but had the gormless mouth and docile jaw of a Swedish tennis star. He had neither seen nor heard of Clarke since he and Sarah had moved to London.

There was some odd male territorial chemistry between Kavanagh and Burchell immediately. It signalled about a million years of animal evolution running on the gene clock as the two men stood a few feet apart from one another in the north London shop.

With his woollen, checked shirt and 150-pound boots, legs crossed as he leaned against a four-foot dresser, Burchell felt no need to mask his indifference to the policeman, a Birmingham cop with a risible accent and a not very bright suit.

Radio Three was playing from the dusty cassette recorder that sat on the battered, roll-top desk against the far wall. There was a Bodum of Traidcraft coffee perched on a pine box next to it.

It was all very civilized; the *Guardian* with attitude. Burchell on Pine; Zen and the art of pine stripping; the Never Ending Circle . . . of dressers from Wales into basement kitchens in Highgate.

'Nice day,' insisted Kavanagh, goading the man.

'It's all weather. Sometimes it rains; sometimes it's sunny. It works out,' said Burchell.

Presley glanced at his boss, taken aback by the carpenter's homily.

'Strong stuff, I suppose,' said Kavanagh, implacable, as

he walked towards the stripping tank at the back of the shop.

Burchell's Levis had several small acid-burn holes that had frayed around the edges. 'It's got to be,' said the man.

'I do mine by hand,' said Kavanagh. 'Paint stripper and wire wool.'

He'd never stripped a door in his life.

'Oh, yes,' said the man, deeply uninterested.

Only Presley looked at his boss with some surprise, impressed by his casual lying, but even more so by the inspector knowing that you *might* use wire wool to strip paint.

'Takes forever,' said the inspector, as he ran his palm down a pair of Victorian shutters. 'No matter. If a job's worth doing . . . eh?'

Kavanagh sauntered down the corridor formed by the stacks of upright doors on either side of him, every half-dozen or so separated by a batten.

He stood at the entrance to the back room and, without turning, spoke into it. 'I had one done in one of these once.' He looked down at the galvanized bath. 'Acid warped it. Glue came out. All the joints came loose.'

'Oh, yes?' said the man.

'Yes,' said the inspector.

'It's *alkaline*, actually,' said the man.

'Sorry?' said Kavanagh, not even turning as the conversational snare dropped over the Scotsman.

'Everyone thinks it's acid. But it's not. Acid would burn the wood.'

'And this strips the stuff just the same?' said Kavanagh, binding the man up.

Burchell rolled his Samson tobacco into a loose cigarette. 'If you do it slowly. The cowboys heat it up . . . then it'll do it in an hour. But your eyes and nose and ears'll be running, and it can explode. There've been a few.'

'But not this?' said the policeman.

'All you need is a fresh mix now and again,' he said.

143

A few bubbles came to the surface, as if confirming the man's assertion.

They'd had their opening skirmish. An away win, Kavanagh reckoned.

'Did you want something? I've got things to do,' said Burchell tetchily.

'Sorry. You carry on,' said Kavanagh, inhaling deeply, but not moving. 'I love the smell in these places. The glue and the wood shavings, all that stuff. Don't you?'

'I can take it or leave it,' said Burchell.

'Umm. I like it. Do you like it, sergeant?' laboured Kavanagh.

'Yes, sir. I love the smell,' replied Presley dutifully.

'Perhaps we'd better let you get on,' said the inspector, but in fact peered intently at the Birmingham maker's name etched into the brass spring on an old pub door. 'If you hear anything about Mr Clarke, you know, like they say in the films, "give us a call", would you? No one ever does, of course. It's just film talk.'

The man resented the baiting, took refuge in smarting silence.

'You must've noticed,' pursued the inspector relentlessly, 'they say: "Give us a call," and they give them a card. Thing is, I've never seen anyone with a card. Well, the Commissioner, Sir Paul Condon, has a card, I'm sure. But people like me. No one at the station has ever said to me, "Would you like a card, Inspector?" Much less, "What sort would you like? Embossed? Serrated edge? A bit of colour?" Nothing. Anyway, give us a ring if anything comes up.'

Presley had his hand on the door handle. There was vandal wire over the thick glass. 'Trouble with break-ins?' said Kavanagh.

'Kids.'

'There's nothing for them here, is there?' said Kavanagh, genuinely interested.

144

'For kicks. They smash it for kicks. No jobs; idle hands . . .' Burchell replied superciliously.

He made the local unemployment sound as if it was Kavanagh's fault.

'I see,' said the inspector, and walked back the few paces towards the big, zinc bath. Presley released the door handle and felt the springs inside the lock return.

Kavanagh nodded towards the leather apron hung on a six-inch nail from a joist. 'You have to watch yourself, I suppose?'

'Yes. You said,' replied the man.

Kavanagh peered into the bath. There was silence between the three men. A few bubbles came to the surface as a door, perhaps a hundred years old, and made from a tree planted a hundred before that, released from some sliver of grain the air that had been trapped there one day two hundred years ago.

'May I?' he asked politely, as he picked up a broom handle made smooth by a thousand immersions.

The man shrugged. Kavanagh pushed up his jacket sleeve, undid the button on his shirt cuff, and pushed the blue cotton up as far as it would go.

He drew the handle through the liquid, watched it creep up the porous pole as he trawled it through the tub.

He traced the outline of the panelled door that lay on the bottom, zigzagged slowly through the quietly fizzing liquid. When he reached the end of the tub, he turned and smiled at Burchell.

'It's bubbling,' he said, gauche.

'It's a fresh mix,' said the man. 'That's why it's bubbling.'

Kavanagh's fanciful notion of air trapped for a century or two flew out of the window.

'Was there something else?' said the man insolently.

Kavanagh looked at him. Presley saw something in that look that was no longer playful irritation. It was loathing, hatred.

The inspector continued to look at the Scotsman, opened his fingers, and let the pole bob on the surface of the mixture. 'No, nothing else,' he said.

From the window of the first-floor flat, Sarah Hardy watched as they walked away towards the Camden Road.

She didn't know a Mercedes from a Mitsubishi, and anyway, what would an old, dark blue Volvo have meant to her, its nose just around the corner in Hargrave Place, its driver slumped down in the fabric-covered seat?

19

Kavanagh and Presley picked up a couple of faxes from their hotel in Melton Street. British Rail had completed their technical investigation of the carriage door from which Adam Curtiss had fallen to his death. It was in perfect working order.

There was news on the Volvo, too. Enhancement of the video-surveillance tape taken from the garage near to the scene of Terry Sugar's murder had isolated the last two letters and one of the digits on the number plate. It had been enough to establish, via an elimination trace and lots of expensive police-hours, the last registered ownership of the car.

A description of the driver was less helpful: he was tallish and slim, but there was no prospect of a positive identification from the shaky images on the tape.

The 'W' registered car had been traded in to a Honda dealer on the south coast two months ago. The dealer had told the police that it was in reasonable nick, but far too old to be dropped in amongst the Preludes and Accords on the forecourt. (And anyway, the Japanese franchisers were inclined to inscrutability when it came to Swedish – or any other nation's – cars sharing their forecourt tarmac.)

The following Thursday, therefore, a junior salesman had driven the blue 244 down to the local auction at Hythe.

It went through at three hundred and seventy pounds.

The car was still MOT'd and had a couple of months' tax on it. Someone had picked up a bargain. The buyer had paid cash and given a name and address in nearby Folkestone. They were false.

Kavanagh was delighted. Someone buys a car in a false name on the south coast. The car is subsequently identified on video at a garage near a double murder in Shropshire. What is almost certainly the same car has a 'Do not park here, please' message left on its windscreen by a Pooter-like resident round the corner from the murders.

A few weeks later, a similar car is identified by a pensioner a couple of hundred yards from where John Lacey is stabbed to death.

Details of the Volvo were circulated to police forces throughout Britain. Identify vehicle and report. Approach driver, who may be armed, with extreme caution.

As the two men sat in the back of their cab and drove out towards Adam Curtiss's flat in Finsbury Park, Kavanagh had a quiet sense of satisfaction: things were starting to come together, the hunches paying off; his notion of a link, based initially on no more than the apparently motiveless murders of Lacey, the Sugars, and then Curtiss, had been confirmed by Sarah Hardy's story. Now, it seemed that the perpetrator of at least two of those killings was the driver of the Volvo saloon.

The inquiry's initial, tentative flicker, originally no brighter than a Turkish match was, remarkably, still glowing.

This glow, this feeling of beginning to tie up the ends, like filling in the last clue of the crossword, or placing the last piece of the jigsaw, was one of the huge pleasures. He had all but forgotten it.

But the very thought process, the slight sense of congratulation, the hubris of acknowledging pleasant things remembered, brought surging in its wake other thoughts, thoughts and feelings of deep pain, regret and loss.

148

He was undone. When having an injection, think of something nice: Mediterranean beaches; peaches and cream.

When fighting back nausea, the heaving, irresistible need to vomit in a public place, think of something other than greasy food, the alcohol swilling in your belly.

Trying *not* to think of his ex-wife, he was back in the sticky web of the emotional net. But before it had ensnared him anew, he had glimpsed for a second the possibility of freedom from this loop of pain. The notion of a life without the constant, accompanying memory of the past. Seen again the possibilities of savouring the unremarkable, the humdrum, the simple joy of life.

Life was not about the 'big moments': the pools win; the foreign holiday; the cup finals of one's life. It was about the quiet satisfaction, the moments of easy content, the space around the edges, space in which to be, to watch, to listen, to moan about the football and the government and, yes, the crime rate.

His fear was that those unremarkable times were much harder to realize than any of the big set pieces. It was little snippets of evanescing nothing that haunted him, rather than the 'special' occasions of their life together: a cup of tea in a motorway café; the smile on a holiday photograph; picking blackberries; even, once, making jam together.

But maybe the glimpse was a beginning. Time is the healer. That's what they said. Everybody did. Bad backs; smoking; diet; divorce. Everybody had a point of view.

Takes between one and five years to get over the separation and divorce of a long marriage; you can fit everyone in the world on to the Isle of Wight; if you join all the buses in London end to end . . . ; on aeroplanes, the pilot and copilot always eat different meals; if everyone in China were to jump up and down at the same time; it takes between one and five years to get over a . . .

Any club that . . .

It was no good peering over the edge. You had to let go. That was the whole point. Suck it and see. It was no good just *looking* at that curious, dimpled shape: smelling might give a clue, peering hard at the heart-shaped, speckled fruit might help, but you had to taste the giving, watery flesh, release the indescribable flavour onto your salivating tongue, bite into the flesh, and it was done.

The taste was in your mouth: strawberry or Paraquat. And then it *was* too late. It was there for ever. No going back. Over the ledge, free fall, no parachute, into the abyss.

He became aware that Presley was speaking to him. His sergeant was looking at him, really looking *at* him. Was he reading his thoughts? Often, these days, Kavanagh was not sure whether he was merely thinking, or actually *saying* his thoughts.

A dispatch rider skimmed their cab as it wove through the traffic on Seven Sisters Road. Presley relieved the pressure of the moment between the two men. 'We'd better get a result on this one, 'cause there's no fucking way *we're* gonna make a living down here delivering pizzas!'

They were into Green Lanes, Greek and Turkish Green Lanes; Thessaloniki or Istanbul: plate-glass windowed 'football clubs' at which, certainly, no football was played.

There were massage parlours, and tobacconists selling lottery tickets, and travel agents, and banks with darkened windows and standing fans, uselessly cooling the chilly, London air.

Every other shop was a greengrocer's, with displays of melons and beans, pineapples and aubergines that spilled onto the pavements. Deep inside, little groups of men chatted, and the girl at the till sold bleach and plastic buckets and light bulbs and toothpaste, just as if it were a dark shop in the quiet backstreets of Athens at three in

150

the boiling afternoon, with *their* smells of soap and cheese and beef tomatoes and apricots.

At Endymion Road the thickset, silver-haired Greek landlord was waiting for the policemen in his Mercedes. During the last few days he had become very short-tempered about the place not yet being available for reletting. It had been sealed by the police since the Buddhist's death, 'pending further inquiries', but it had been nearly two weeks now, and the landlord was threatening an official complaint.

Mr Stassios showed the policemen Curtiss's former flat. He had never met his tenant: he owned half a dozen houses dotted around the Finsbury area and had a letting agent who dealt with the plumbing and the collection of his considerable rents.

While the policemen made a quiet progress through the flat and looked for clues to the sudden, violent death of the erstwhile tenant, the owner conducted an equally careful study of the window frames, carpets and general decorative order of his property.

It was a bare and nearly empty place; not sterile, but calm and ordered. One bunch of flowers had wilted and died on the uncluttered mantelpiece. There was a little shrine in the bedroom with a heavy bronze Buddha on a white napkin, and two incense holders with several burned-down sticks in each one. There were copies of the *Bhagavadgita* and the Upanishads on the floor near the prayer mat before the altar.

Even with the big, Greek landlord puffing from room to quiet room, there was an immutable quiet about the whole place: letters were filed, socks folded one into the other in the sock drawer; shirts were on hangers, towels neatly folded and stacked in the airing cupboard.

The kitchen was tidy, with the few utensils and crockery that had last been used placed on a tea-towel on the draining board with another tea towel covering them.

On the shelves were a few travel books, numerous religious and philosophical texts, and a couple of modern novels. Maybe the man didn't hoard much; maybe the whole notion of acquisition and possessions was alien to his religious beliefs.

The policemen took a few letters and bank statements (his address book and wallet had been with him when he had died, and were already in the possession of the police). Kavanagh told the landlord that he could let the flat again as soon as Curtiss's mother had collected the rest of his things.

He bid the man kalimera, and Mr Stassios, charmed by the policeman's use of the word, shook his hand warmly and bid them farewell.

20

As well as quarrying slate and being something of a railway centre, the little Welsh town of Machynlleth had manufactured snuff and supported a printing industry in the late-nineteenth century.

It had then had a hiatus of half a century or more when it slipped from view, the itinerants moving on, to build their railways and father their illegitimate children elsewhere.

But during the last two or three decades, the nostalgia industry had arrived with a vengeance in mid-Wales, and the High Street, once a sombre, almost gloomy, place, populated only by grocers and hardware merchants, butchers and outfitters, quite suddenly sprouted half a dozen 'craft' shops. Places selling socks and bonnets, cardigans and egg cups; love spoons, and all things Welsh; a hundred things in slate, from clocks and barometers, to maps of Montgomeryshire etched on half-inch-thick stone.

These people had come to retailing late, and they approached it with an evangelical fervour, clasping to their collective bosom the new-found deity of mammon, and competing zealously for worshippers at their gift-shop shrines.

Even the Hebron chapel now displayed an orange fascia board, four feet deep and thirty feet long, that obscured the original benefactors' names and proclaimed, not the

Word of a stern God, but *Bedroom quality carpet: £2.99 a square yard.*

The dour shopkeepers took the money and barely smiled, as if any levity on their part might betray their suspicion that their new-found labours were little more than fraud.

Machynlleth's disenfranchised youngsters, meanwhile, scorned the immigrants and tourists, and refused to move aside for them on the crowded market-day pavements of their town.

Sat sourly in the Black Lion, two hundred yards down the road from the Owain Glendower Centre (home, once, to the rebel prince's fifteenth-century Assembly, now a tourist attraction for the gawping trippers from Dudley and West Bromwich), they greeted with a frosty silence any stranger from the Midlands who might, haplessly, wander into their last stronghold on the edge of town.

On the way to Dolgellau, a couple of miles up the valley, was the other reason for Machynlleth's new-found celebrity: the Centre of Alternative Technology, an experiment in 'sustainable living', had been started by a right-thinking, head-screwed-on type in the early seventies.

No woolly-headed, acid-brained hippy this: Gerard Morgan Grenville had seen the light on the road, not to Damascus, but a deeply inauspicious slate quarry on the A487.

The Centre plodded on throughout the muddled seventies, but it was during the ozone-heady days of the eighties that it had soared in popularity and become a sort of low-tech Alton Towers, attracting ninety thousand visitors each year.

Briony Clarke was a clone of her mother: an inch or two taller, a younger figure, but the same long, fair hair; the big, slightly surprised brown eyes; the straight nose. They were sisters, born twenty years apart.

She welcomed them into the little house in Heol Pentrerhedyn, Machynlleth's main street, made herb tea, and brought in a plate of biscuits.

The men were big in the cosy room with its amiable clutter of packed bookshelves, magazines and papers, tapes and CDs. There was no evidence of any other occupant; in the porch was a pair of wellington boots and a nice pair of greased walking boots, but they were both size fives, Kavanagh reckoned; maybe a six, but no bigger. Inside the boots were walking socks: thick, red, woollen ones, neatly tucked and folded.

As she poured the tea the young woman chatted in an open, friendly manner, small talk about the weather and their train journey.

'And have you been here long?' asked Presley.

'About six months,' she said. 'I'm doing a year at the Centre. I'm studying environmental science at university.'

Kavanagh was glad to be listening to someone who volunteered information. He spent his life dragging sentences out of monosyllabics, people who either didn't want to talk, for fear of incriminating themselves, or were unable to, through a lack of nurturing.

'It's about your father, Briony,' said Presley.

'Yes, my mum phoned last night and told me.'

'Have you seen him recently?' asked the sergeant.

'No,' she said. 'He hasn't been in touch for ages. The last time I saw him was just before he went abroad.'

'When was that?'

'I can't remember exactly, but it was in the spring, early spring, about the time I came up here. Mum was in London with . . .'

The girl felt uneasy speaking the name of her mother's new partner. Kavanagh approved. These days, he valued fidelity above all things.

'Burchell? Peter Burchell?' helped Kavanagh.

'Yes. Peter Burchell.'

'Don't you get on with him?' asked the inspector.

155

'It's not that,' she said. 'Not really. It's just difficult. Mum, Dad. You know. You can't just see your mum with someone else like that. I couldn't anyway. It didn't seem fair to Dad. It seemed . . . I don't know, it's silly I suppose, like I was being a traitor. But it isn't Mum's fault. She's entitled to . . . whatever it is she wants.'

'Yes, of course,' said Kavanagh. 'Where did he go, your dad?'

'He had a friend in Italy. A friend from years back. They'd always kept in touch. From university, I think. He wanted to get away. He didn't seem to be getting over things. As time went on, he was getting worse, not better. I think he thought it might help him.'

Kavanagh was chary of hearing about time's *not* being a healer.

'Go on,' he said, bracing himself.

'Since he and Mum split up, he just seemed to fall apart. He found it hard. He'd always seen himself as strong in the relationship, and because of that, it was a much worse thing for him than it was for her. To be honest, I think it was liberating for her.'

Kavanagh winced.

'It happens. Women are in marriages and their husband dies or whatever, and suddenly the woman finds that all this mystique that had to surround paying the electricity bill and the mortgage, or getting a new tyre for the car . . . it's just that: mystique.'

He listened, sipped his bitter raspberry tea.

'I shouldn't generalize,' she offered, conciliatory. 'Every situation's different, of course. And it wasn't Dad's fault. It was *his* upbringing and conditioning; *his* parents and all, I suppose.'

Kavanagh watched the pretty girl's lips moving. She had her long hair piled on top of her head in a way that intrigued him. There was a neat plait up the back of her neck, which then disappeared into the mass of fair hair that was bunched there.

156

As a teenager, he had often got on well with his girl-friends' mothers. Now, it seemed, he had reached an age where he was destined to court the mothers while actually mesmerized by their daughters.

'When they split up, Dad went to pieces, just got worse and worse.'

'In what way?' said Kavanagh.

'He'd always been a bit obsessive. About his job, about his writing. Everything had to be done, whatever it was, no matter how small, right then. Just so; there and then.

'I've never been like that,' she gestured to her cluttered room. 'His life was full of little routines and habits that he had. So tiny things seemed huge, insurmountable.

'When they broke up, all that fell apart, and he was lost.'

'And?' said Kavanagh.

'He knew, deep down, that their parting had to be. It had to be, and now, here it was. He said he didn't "own" her. He had a kind of strength. A sense of moral right. But he also knew it was against *nature*.'

She paused. 'You know about the baby?'

Kavanagh nodded.

'He knew he had wronged her, but because of that, I think he believed that he had to let her go, even though it was destroying him.'

The three of them sat quietly for a few moments.

'So, what happened next?' said Kavanagh.

'She'd got involved with Peter.'

'Yes,' said Kavanagh.

'Dad tried to be rational and contained. He moved to a flat in Chester: new life; carried on with his writing, he always did that, no matter what.'

'A new book?' asked the inspector.

'Yes, a novel. It was the material *for* a book. One day, he said, he'd write it.'

'Did he show it to you?' asked Presley.

157

'He never showed anybody anything he was working on,' she said.

'Why not?' asked the policeman.

'He said that if you talked about stuff before you wrote it, you had no excitement in doing it, you'd talked it out of your system and you couldn't then be bothered to write it.'

'I see,' said Kavanagh. 'Please, carry on.'

'They were selling the house. I used to go and see Dad in his flat in Chester. The place was a mess. It was terrible to see. He never used to live like that.

'Mum got more involved with . . . you know, Peter. Dad was always thinking about Mum, talking about the past, what they'd had, and what they had lost.

'But it was *him* that had lost everything, really. She was all right.

'He'd talk about their past, things and people I'd never heard of. How she'd made him unhappy. These things were always on his mind, he'd just go round and round them, over and over again. He said it was only his writing that kept him sane. He was obsessed with their past.

'She told him to stop writing letters to her. He had started to threaten her with what he thought was his love, but was really just a kind of jealousy. He was drinking heavily, and not sleeping properly.

'He wanted to put back the clock, and I told him: You can't do that. It's past. That time has gone. But he couldn't accept it.

'And he has that writer thing: I think people such as him, they save up the moments, the good times and the bad times, for use in the future.

'If he'd *lived* the moment, kissed "the joy as it flies", as Mum used to say, it might have been different.'

After a long silence, she said. 'What has he done? Mum said it was serious.'

'We don't know, Briony. But it *is* serious, and we do need to speak to him, urgently.'

'Why?'

'Did your mother not tell you any more?'

'She said it involved people from her past.'

Kavanagh looked at Presley. The herb tea was cold beside him on the floor.

Presley said, 'Several people have died recently. They were known to your mother. It could be that your father is involved.'

'I see,' she said, not suggesting for even a moment that the notion was anything but reasonable.

'So, the last time you heard from your father was when?' asked Kavanagh.

'Ages. Three months at least. Just a postcard.'

'Have you got it?'

'Yes. And a few things were sent on to me from his flat in Chester. Do you want those, too?'

'Yes, we're going over there to have a look. Anything that'll help us locate him. Do you have the address of his friend in Italy?'

'Yes, of course.'

The card had been posted in Milan, and had a picture of the Duomo on it. There were several buff envelopes, social security ones, and a dozen bits of junk mail.

They declined her offer of more tea, shook hands and left her with instructions about contacting them if her father got in touch.

21

The policemen stood on the platform beside a couple of middle-aged hikers as the Chester train, a single-carriage affair, rocked into the station.

The walkers were serious people: thigh-length Gore-Tex jackets, small rucksacks neatly attached to their backs, map pouches on nylon cord around their necks.

The Machynlleth residents, off to Chester for some early Christmas shopping, were conspicuous by their track-suit bottoms, Naf Naf tops and trainers.

As soon as they were boarded, Presley went through the social security envelopes. They were markedly short of revelations: a Giro-cheque, followed by several letters explaining the Department of Social Security's cessation of payment of benefit to Jeff Clarke.

The only signs that Clarke had ever lived at the big, rambling house on the outskirts of Chester were the bits of mail that sat on the hall stand in the once grand, now rather run down, Victorian house.

He may well have been murdering people during the last few weeks, but Clarke was being offered loans, hospital and health care insurance, extra credit cards and the opportunity to buy a time share in Scotland. He was also, according to Reader's Digest, only a few numbers away from winning a hundred thousand pounds and a new Ford Escort.

Before Kavanagh could open the only piece of personal

post, a white Conqueror envelope with a second-class stamp, but addressed to Clarke in his full name and with the appendage 'Esq.' after his surname, the girl who had moved into his former room returned from work.

She showed them the room. She and her boyfriend had painted it the first week that she had been there. It was bright and cheerful and the youngster stood awkwardly beside the two policemen as they looked down at the collection of fluffy toys that sat ranged at the top of her bed.

The former tenant had left his sheets and towels and a few books and lots of papers: 'Pages and pages of writing, some longhand, some typed, chapters from a book. It was like a diary. I didn't read much of it. I like Catherine Cookson. I've got them all.' She gestured to her shelves and the popular author's books ranged there.

'What did you do with his things?'

'I kept them all for weeks, in cardboard boxes and plastic sacks, but eventually I put them out for the dustbin men.' She felt guilty. 'There's not much room here.'

'Of course,' said Kavanagh.

He looked through the sash window into the garden. Amongst the big trees and hydrangea bushes were the remnants of an iron fence that had once divided the house from the nearby fields.

Now, on the other side of the boundary, there were a dozen 'executive' houses with double garages and smooth, tarmac drives.

The policemen thanked the girl and wandered through the house, tapping on doors and speaking to the students and office workers who lived there.

A boy of nineteen on the first floor remembered the man who had lived, briefly, at the back of the house. He'd passed him in the hall, said hello. 'And then one day he was gone. I never heard any music or anything. He had a girl come sometimes. Could have been his daughter, I guess. About the right age, anyway. He looked rough. I always thought he was having a bad time.

'There's sometimes quite a bit of noise here, at weekends, or when people come back from the pub, but he never complained. Never said a word.

'Was he alcoholic? There were always bottles clanking out to the bin, and Thresher's carrier bags around. Why? What's happened to him?'

'Thanks, son, we'll be in touch if we need you. Thanks a lot.'

It was just after opening time and they sat amongst the other, miserable, Happy Hour customers at a pub down the road from the big house.

Kavanagh opened the envelope carefully, peeling back the stuck fold with barely a tear of the woven, quality paper.

Dear Mr Clarke,
Thank you for sending us your typescript, *Words of Comfort*.

I would like to say immediately that your book is infinitely better than the vast majority of unsolicited typescripts that we receive in this office and, indeed, in other circumstances, I might well have been able to make an offer to represent you.

However, as I am sure you know, the market is, at present, in a very depressed state, and only those books that we feel one hundred per cent confident of placing can we take on.

You write well and your book has good atmosphere but, at the end of the day, the domestic nature of the story is perhaps too depressing and downbeat for today's market.

Also, I feel you should try to bear in mind that readers generally want a hero or, at the very least, someone with whom they can identify. Your book, with its vengeful protagonist, markedly lacks anyone who could be thus described.

I hope these comments are not too unhelpful, and I wish you every success in placing your book with either another agent or direct with a publisher.

There was a PS.

It is, of course, essential that the senders of unsolicited typescripts submit return postage with their work. Given the very high costs involved, GouldThomas Associates are unable to return your novel unless you forward five pounds to cover these costs.

If we do not hear from you within six weeks, we will have no alternative but to dispose of your typescript.

The letter was over two months old.

Kavanagh and Presley were waiting outside the door of the literary agency's third-floor office on Manchester's Oxford Street at nine o'clock the following morning.

Neither man felt that he looked like a writer, and it was difficult to imagine that authors travelled in twos, but Mrs Copeland, the formidable receptionist, had become adept at dealing with any number of deceptions perpetrated by those wily writers who, at all costs, would *see* the agent, as if their written words alone were not sufficient testimony to their worth.

Eventually, convinced of their story, and finding about them nothing bulkier than warrant cards, she admitted the policemen and made them coffee.

Henry Gould arrived twenty minutes later.

A man in his mid-fifties, wearing brogues and an Austin Reed three-piece suit, he showed them into his office.

He apologized for the chaos and moved books and typescripts from a couple of chairs so that the men might sit down.

His desk was covered with clients' folders, correspondence, faxes and contracts. Every other available surface, and much of the carpet, was obscured by manuscripts. Even as they spoke, the receptionist brought in that morning's mail, including another four chunky parcels.

'It's about a manuscript that was sent to you recently . . .' began Kavanagh.

'Yes?' said Gould.

'It was sent to you by someone called Clarke, Jeff Clarke.'

'The name rings a bell,' said Gould as Kavanagh passed the agent's letter across to the man.

'Oh, yes. I remember it. Good book. Well, not so much a good *book* as a good *writer*. Powerful prose. What's he done?'

'We don't know. We don't even know what's *in* the book yet. Do you still have it?'

Gould glanced down at the date on the letter and, without answering, spoke into the internal telephone on his desk. 'Mrs Copeland, could you check whether a manuscript by one Jeff Clarke has been returned, or whether we still have it, please?

'Yes, as I say,' continued Gould, unprompted, 'it was a well-written book. Claustrophobic and intensely felt, written from within. No car chases, no drugs money.' He raised his eyebrows a millimetre. 'Not at all suitable for most of today's readers, I'm afraid. Of over five hundred unsolicited books that we were offered last year, we took only two. Mr Jeff Clarke's came close to being the first this year.'

Mrs Copeland knocked and entered. 'I'm afraid he didn't send a remittance. I put out all of July to September's typescripts only last week. You did *ask* me to, Mr Gould.'

'Of course, Jane. It's perfectly all right. That's all for now, thank you.' And the woman left the room.

'Sorry,' said Gould. 'We have to be very strict.' He gestured with his hand around the room. 'If authors don't forward the postage, we just don't have the room. After six weeks . . . I know it sounds awful, but believe me, it is the only way. She simply puts them out for the paper-recycling chaps every three months.'

'I see,' said Kavanagh. 'Do you remember much about the book? The actual *story*?'

Gould read his own letter again.

'Yes, I remember it,' said the agent. 'Murders, motivated by things that had happened in the past.'

'What kind of things?' said Kavanagh.

'Infidelity. His wife had been unfaithful. And now the narrator had to erase all of that past by killing her ex-lovers.'

'I see,' said Kavanagh. 'And the wife? What of her?'

'Yes, in the end, her too,' said Gould.

'How did he kill the victims?' said Presley.

'One person was strangled, another garroted, another knifed. They were low-tech murders. No fancy machines, not even firearms. Just the brutal, messy murder that a man alone can do: a kitchen knife, a piece of wire, that sort of thing.

'The killings were not remarkable in themselves. There's worse on television every night. But they were realistic. It was real death. Real murder. It was *felt*.

'And now you're telling me he's doing these things?' continued Gould.

'We are certainly very concerned,' said the inspector, with some understatement.

'They say everybody's got a book in them!' said Presley, as the two men hurried through Manchester city centre towards the railway station.

'Yes, that's what they say,' said Kavanagh. 'He tried to

165

get it out of his system in the book. It didn't work. And now he's doing it. What he "needs" to do to get clear of his past.'

Kavanagh thought, yet again, of his troubled sleep the previous night in their Manchester hotel. He had woken several times to thoughts of Rachael. To call them dreams would have been to suggest a distance that simply did not exist.

Once, although the days had been difficult, often very difficult, the booze-sodden nights had offered a few hours' respite.

Now, he was like a tissue, a paper towel whose absorbency had been surfeited, and he spilled over. He approached sleep with a macabre fascination, as his subconscious presented to his defenceless mind the images that, during the daylight hours, he wilfully stifled.

'Different murders, though,' said Presley.

'Yes. Not the same methods, of course,' said Kavanagh. 'You know, Kev, he's not *mad* . . .'

Presley glanced at his boss as they weaved along the crowded pavements, but there was no sign of a smile there.

'And his missis, and her bloke?' said Presley. 'They're next?'

'Yes, them next,' said Kavanagh, with a singular lack of feeling.

22

There wasn't a train to London for half an hour. Kavanagh ordered them tea and a sandwich while Presley went down the platform and phoned London.

Suddenly the sergeant was back, leaning over the formica table. 'They've found the car. A good copper. Sharp eyes. The car was filthy, knackered, but the plates were clean, brand new. They've checked it out. It's our man's.'

'Where?' asked Kavanagh.

'Tufnell Park,' said Presley.

'Where the fuck's Tufnell Park?' said Kavanagh. 'Is it near Brecknock Road?'

'Right next door,' said Presley. 'The car's half a mile from where they're doing the stakeout on the flat.'

'What about the surveillance?' asked the inspector.

'They say there's been no movement: no lights, nothing. He's knocked, but there's no answer. He doesn't think there's anyone in. They want to know if we've got the details right, and whether they've got to continue staking it out.'

'Have they phoned?'

'Yes. No reply. They want to know whether we want them to do a forced.'

Kavanagh looked down the platform. 'Tell them we're on our way. Just keep watching the place. Don't do anything. We'll be there as soon as we can. Just keep watching.'

*   *   *

At Euston, they were met by a uniformed officer who sped them through the parting traffic on a blue light and sirens. The driver brought them up through Kentish Town and slowed at Raveley Street where two officers were standing beside the blue Volvo, plastic 'Police' tape stretched all around it.

As they entered the bottom end of Brecknock Road, their driver turned off his blue light and drew up behind a 'B' registered Ford, parked fifty yards down from the flat.

The sergeant charged with watching Sarah Hardy's home was hunched up in the dirty, grey, smoke-filled Sierra. Presley and Kavanagh clambered into the car with the unshaven man. If he was on undercover duty, it was working: he'd more likely get hired as a minicab driver or picked up for kerb crawling than be identified as a policeman.

'When did you get here?' asked the inspector.

'This morning; nine o'clock.'

'And what about yesterday?'

'Who knows?' he said.

'Well, who did you take over from? He must have given you an update?'

'There *was* no one yesterday. I was the first shift. They couldn't get anyone over here. We'd got more on than a domestic yesterday: fucking bombs going off in the City.

'Everyone available was called in and redrafted. I've been on shift thirty-six hours already. I only came over here as a favour.'

'Sorry, mate. Cheers,' said Kavanagh.

The cop flashed him a look through half-closed eyes, looking for the signs of irony. He was ready to tell him what to do with his surveillance job, inspector or not, but there was nothing there. Kavanagh's gratitude was genuine.

'You going in?' asked the sergeant. 'There's no one there. I've been watching: no lights, no curtain movement. Nothing at the windows. I've knocked a couple of times; phoned twice.' He gestured to the mobile in the parcel shelf. 'Nothing. What are they anyway? My gaffer said something about a jealous husband. It's not one of these holding his missis up and us having to cordon the street off is it? 'Cause I'll never get home. He'll want a bleedin' helicopter or something. They always want a fucking helicopter these days, and then we'll all be here for a week!'

Kavanagh was warming to the sergeant. The Met. were an entirely different bunch. A race apart. Stereotypes *did* apply: Brummies: lowlifers; terrible accents; car dealers. Welsh: tightfisted; anti-English, whining. Londoners: criminals; back of a lorry; sell their mother; knew the score.

The job was different down here: much more crime; so much more violence. These blokes were a law unto themselves, a force within a force, different rules, different behaviour. Men and women who were barely containing a volatile city. It was more New York than Birmingham.

'It's a bit more than a domestic,' said Kavanagh. And then, hopefully, 'Or maybe it's nothing at all. Who knows? Me and Elvis'll go and have a look. You hang on here. Why not get yourself a cup of tea or something? We'll be all right for a bit.'

'Cheers. I'll just close them for a few minutes. That's what I need. Give us a nudge when you get back.'

They passed the shop and peered through the vandal wire on the door. The place looked exactly the same: the same bits of furniture; the radio cassette on the roll-top desk. There were a couple of bits of post on the floor inside the door. The shop hadn't been opened today, at least.

They walked the few yards to the street door of the flat. It had the standard burglar-deterrent solidity about it; Presley put his shoulder against it, but there was absolutely no movement. The two Chubb deadlocks and the centre mortice saw to that. Bring back *The Sweeney*, thought Kavanagh: when John Thaw and Dennis Waterman took a run at doors, they flew off their hinges.

Presley peered into the letter box, but could see nothing. He pressed his ear to the opening, but could hear nothing above the noise of the traffic thundering by.

'What do you reckon?' said Kavanagh.

'She'd have said if she was going away. Especially with us telling her to be careful and that we'd have the place watched. We can't leave without checking it out, and her nutter ex-husband's car parked down the road.'

'Do we break it down, or what?' said Kavanagh, seeking to abdicate his responsibility, and feeling less confident than usual on this alien turf.

'Fuck knows,' said Elvis, declining his boss's offer to share the initiative.

The sergeant was sleeping in the front seat of the car, his mouth wide open. They woke him and he punched the buttons on his mobile, handing the phone to Presley when he had got through.

Presley described the type and number of the locks on the solid sapele door and the Paddington CID desk arranged to have a locksmith up to them within the hour.

The locksmith arrived in a little Honda Acty van and began his work as he delivered a monologue about his work. He broke in for the police all the time. Burglar alarms that went off while residents were away on holiday; premises having to be secured after raids or break-ins. There was nothing that the man hadn't seen.

He fiddled with half a dozen keys before opening the three separate locks. The whole thing took less than five minutes. He handed them the keys so that they could lock up again when they left, took a signature from Kavanagh on his job invoice, handed the inspector the yellow copy, and disappeared down the road.

*　　*　　*

The two men stood at the bottom of the stairs and listened. Kavanagh reckoned he could look at an opaque bottle or a paint tin and, just by looking at it, tell whether there was anything in it. Houses were the same. The very knock on the door felt different if there was someone in the house; the carpet on the floor transmitted a sense of someone's presence if another person's feet were pressed into the pile.

They climbed the steep stairs, one hand on the rail, heads peering upwards towards the low-wattage light bulb that hung there.

Kavanagh's hand touched something sticky on the bannister. He lifted his hand and slowly opened the palm to examine the smudge of blood there.

He showed the thin, red, veiny sight to Presley. Neither man spoke. At the top of the stairs a coat was lying on the floor. It was one thing, a nothing, but it was everything. Both men had seen enough to know the difference between a coat dropped randomly in the hall after a late night out, and the same coat lying there after violence. A car parked badly, compared with one abandoned by joyriders at the side of the road. A body lying inert on the floor: the odd, always surprising fold of the body, the incongruity of the limbs, the awkwardness and absence of vanity that accompanied death.

The sitting-room door where they had spoken to Sarah Hardy a day earlier was ajar. Kavanagh pushed it very gently with the tips of his fingers. Fools rush in . . . The blood on his hand was sticky at the base of his fingers.

His eyes swept the scene, took in the general, ignored the particular, filed that in his brain for later, in five seconds' time.

Little disarray; same room as before; a big moon waxing through the net curtains; the glow of a streetlamp illuminating the scene. In the corner, away from the window, a man in a low chair. Knife.

The man looked back at them as they stood in the door-

171

way. His eyes revealed nothing. Without a reaction, it was impossible to gauge the situation. Without a reaction, that *was* the situation. No blink. No emotion. No interest. But in his hand, a long knife.

No one spoke. Was he a lunger? Would they be able to get down the stairs and out of the front door before being wedged in the narrow passageway, knife thrusts raining down upon them, nothing to protect them except their outstretched, flailing arms?

The man was inert. His very stillness was frightening. How long had he been sitting here? They had blown it. They had been foolhardy, entered the premises unarmed and understrength; no backup, no weapons, no body armour. The Met. would have a laugh about the dopey Brummies on this one.

The man wasn't injured, not as far as Kavanagh could see, but there were dark marks on his jeans; the knife had no reflection on its blade. Was that, too, dulled with the stuff?

Kavanagh wanted desperately to ask: Where is your wife? Where is Peter Burchell? The overwhelming wish to know. The same thing that was making his emotional life a daily torture. The need to know: to be *informed.*

Where were the couple? They were dead, of course. In the bedroom? The kitchen? Where was that?

There were no obvious wounds on the man; perhaps a graze on his forehead, nothing else.

But blood on the carpet? A nice, plain, grey carpet that Kavanagh had tacitly admired yesterday. It was heavily stained.

'Are you all right?' said Kavanagh.

It was about as ridiculous a question as he could have asked. But they couldn't stay here, like this, in this silence, for ever, the man's eyes registering nothing, the carpet stained.

Worst of all, the inspector's hand was horribly sticky,

sticky with someone else's blood. In the midst of this drama, what Kavanagh wanted, more than anything, was to wash his hand.

23

'Are you all right?'

If the question had been redundant at the first time of its asking, it was risible now. But Kavanagh had no idea *what* to say.

In a way, his mind was working well. It was very sharp, very clear; it was entering and processing information with great speed and clarity.

He'd heard all that pseudoscientific nonsense about the human brain's capacity to deal with information; it was pub-bore stuff. Absolutely no use in dealing with the man sitting in the chair ten feet away from him with a knife in his hand and an uncanny lack of feeling in his eyes.

The man in the chair was Jeff Clarke. He bore little resemblance to his pretty daughter. She had taken her looks from her mother. This man was tall and thin, hollow cheeked, gaunt.

He'd killed several people. He didn't look well. An understatement. His wife, his ex-wife, wasn't here. Nor was her lover. Where were *they*?

That guy from Ladbrokes or William Hill who kept popping up at the Booker Prize and on election nights to give the odds: he wouldn't give a good price on Sarah Hardy and Peter Burchell still being alive.

Was this the same knife that had killed John Lacey in Birmingham? Was this the man who had coerced the Sugars into their old car and filled it with carbon monoxide until they had died a gasping, ghastly death? And was this the man who had forced Adam Curtiss from a train doing over a hundred inter-city miles an hour? He was big enough, certainly.

Kavanagh's brain threw up these and a dozen other questions, and all the time he was aware of his colleague's shallow breathing as Presley stood close behind him.

Should he talk some more? Risk another question? Wait for this unpredictable character to speak. Kavanagh didn't want to pressure him, not at all, not in any way.

He was curious, and afraid; terrified, really. But he had to stay sharp.

There was a low, ornamental table between them; perhaps he would be able to kick that in the way of him. He would use the sofa cushions to try and fend off the blows as the man lunged. There was nothing else to hand.

Perhaps Clarke would topple and the two of them would then be able to bundle him down, get that killing blade away from him.

Plans were all right; but it was like girls doing judo classes, or hoku fuku or whatever it was called these days: the bad guys who attacked you in the night didn't do a ceremonial bow and adopt a 'stance'. They grabbed you from behind, cut you, tore off your clothes, stuffed things into you. It wasn't combat by numbers; it was quick and violent, and often deadly.

Maybe Clarke'd bale out of the window: film stuff, Jimmy Cagney nonsense. But Kavanagh knew that life's reality was less spectacular, more prosaic, more ghastly. More Chabrol and Hitchcock: people who didn't die easily, men and women whose limbs refused to fold, whose blood continued inconveniently to pour and drip.

And anyway, smashed through the window, falling twenty feet to his death or a certain coma on the hard Brecknock Road below, wouldn't do; even afraid, Kavanagh didn't want this: too many unanswereds. His fear was balanced by his deep need to *know*. A few hours of question and answer. The whys; the wherefores; the hows and whens that fuelled his motor.

This Othello with the knife, though, he was out of logic. *He* was up for anything. Othello: wrong thought. Rachael: betrayal; loss. Othello: green-eyed monster; jealousy; murder; Iago; bad track.

This was the result. This is where it led; *could* lead. It was powerful stuff, he knew that. He hadn't gone this far, but he'd thought of it. Murder had seemed reasonable.

One time, he'd thought of hanging a sheet from the underpass bridge, like husbands did for their wives on their fortieth birthdays.

But his sheet said, 'Come back, Rachael. *Please* Come Back.' He hadn't done it. But he'd thought it; believed it possible. At four in the morning, it had seemed reasonable.

And he'd prayed she'd die, didn't care how. Just get the fuck dead. Out of my life. Out of my mind. No prospect of being with another, any other. Was *that* so different from this?

It wasn't. He'd thought those things. Love and murderous death. They were an inch, a millimetre, a second's thought apart.

And this was reality, not just a play. *Just* a play? What about the woman in the audience at Stratford who, unable to bear Desdemona's being killed by her husband cried out to the Moor, 'She didn't *do* it; she didn't *do* it.'

He liked that. He liked Desdemona's virtue, and he liked the gauche woman from Michigan or Ohio who was moved to cry out and defend it.

Kavanagh might die. Any second: lunge, dead. Injured: punctured lung; severed arteries; multiple stab wounds.

Two paragraphs in the nationals; a page in the *Camden Express* or whatever: 'While investigating a murder, Detective Inspector Frank Kavanagh was overcome by the suspect and subsequently died from multiple stab wounds.

'The Chief Constable of the West Midlands force, to which the officer was attached, said that Kavanagh, a policeman with nearly twenty years' service, had made an outstanding contribution to the force, and would be deeply missed.

'His estranged wife, Rachael, said that he had given his life to his work.' (She had always appreciated irony, he thought.)

Fucking hell, he could see the cellophane-wrapped floral tributes lining the pavement outside the flat. Talismans of the public's vain hope that their outrage at yet another barbarous killing would arrest the tide of violence that was now endemic throughout the land.

Would injury suffice? Would she be moved to come back? Of course she would *visit*. She would come to his bedside. She didn't hate him. Just didn't love him any more. Was indifferent. That was so much harder.

And if she came, walked into the antiseptic ward, would her man be outside? Out on the green-floored corridor? In the waiting room? In his car in the car park, awaiting her return?

'Are you all right?'

The question was still ringing around the room. The period of silence. Cod psychology. True, though. Whoever spoke first lost the advantage. He knew it. He saw it played daily. It was kids' stuff. To take the advantage. But people *were* kids. *Wanted* an advantage.

Kavanagh didn't want to pressure this man in any way. He wanted him to put down the bloody blade. He'd speak; give up any notion of trying to be in control, remove any idea of threat or advantage; try another question.

'Where are they?'

The man looked up, parted his lips a fraction. He nodded slowly, acknowledging something in the question.

'Your wife? Where is she?' ventured Kavanagh.

Clarke smiled. It wasn't nice. There was an incongruity; the motionless body, the smile.

'I've not been well,' he said. He pushed his hand through his unkempt dark hair. 'Not well.'

177

'No,' said Kavanagh. 'Would you like something? A drink? Some tea?'

He nodded slightly.

Negotiation. Establish rapport. That was what you had to do. He'd been on the course. Watched the movies. Except. Except, of course, where you *didn't* want to be noticed. That was another one, wasn't it? That was the hostage situation. Your crazed Lebanese or Iranian captors were negotiating with the government or whatever. You were stuck in the plane with the Palestinians or on the train with the hooded South Moluccans. Then, you went 'grey'.

The last thing you wanted was to be noticed. You got noticed and then, when they wanted to take someone out, show they meant business, up the ante a little, it was *you* that was the currency.

Your life: your mum and dad's son; somebody's hapless husband/wife/grandfather/daughter, was taken out, shot, and dropped, dead, onto the tarmac.

Don't get noticed. No eye contact. Nothing. Grey. It was *important* not to mix them up. Life endangering.

But now, this situation: rapport. That was what was called for. Rapport. Name of a dating agency. Maybe he'd meet someone one day. Someone he could love, really love, and then Rachael wouldn't matter to him any more; at least not matter to him like she did now.

Rapport. That's what they were getting. The man had said yes to a drink. Kavanagh hadn't thought it through. It meant he was going to be alone with him. Was that worse? He was more vulnerable.

He had created a situation where he was going to be alone with him. Would Presley do something daft? Anything? Would he try and get help and make Kavanagh's plight worse?

The man was waiting. There was a kind of etiquette, a curious sort of propriety. Kavanagh had asked the man if he wanted a drink. The man had said yes. Now he was

178

waiting. It was unlikely he would say, 'Excuse me, but where is my cup of tea?' But he *was* waiting.

'Tea, then?' said Kavanagh.

He nodded.

'OK,' said Frank to his sergeant, 'let's have some tea.'

'You sure?' said Presley.

'Yes. Just easy,' said Kavanagh, quietly.

Presley backed a footstep or two into the hall.

Kavanagh wanted to sit, but was afraid to. He would have less chance of defending himself if the man went for him. He leaned more of his weight against the door pillar. 'Where is your wife?' he asked again, gently.

The suggestion of a mirthless smile came back to Clarke's lips. 'My ex-wife,' he said.

Kavanagh didn't like the ambiguity in the reply: ex-alive, or ex-married? They were dead. He knew it.

'Yes, your ex-wife,' said the inspector.

'Gone,' Clarke eventually said.

'May I go to her?' said Kavanagh. 'She may need help. Perhaps I could help her.'

The man moved his head from side to side. 'No,' he said, with finality.

No, she didn't need help? Or, no, he couldn't help her?

'Is she all right?' said Kavanagh.

There was a tiny movement as his fingers tightened on the hilt of the knife and the dull blade turned very slightly in his hand. Kavanagh backed off.

From the kitchen – remarkable – came the slight sounds of familiar domesticity: cups and saucers and teaspoons, even the insistent bubbling of the electric kettle, and then the click of its shutting off.

The inspector heard the three separate sounds of the water going onto the tea bags in the cups or mugs. Tosser. He never makes it properly, in the pot.

Presley manoeuvred past his boss in the doorway, brought in the three drinks, sugar and milk on a tray.

179

The sergeant gestured to the low table in front of Clarke, and the man moved his head in agreement.

When he had lowered the tray, Presley took one of the mugs of steaming tea, threw it straight at the man's head and followed it by raining down a heavy blow on his face. He moved with greater speed than Kavanagh had ever seen him display before.

It was a second before the inspector realized that it was incumbent upon him, too, to be involved. But the man was barely responding. He had no fight or resistance, the knife had fallen to the floor as he cried out from the pain of the scalding tea. He had received in answer to his cries Presley's big fist which had split his nose and broken his lips and teeth.

Kavanagh picked up the knife; he knew that he lacked the wherewithal to plunge a knife into anyone, but he wanted it well away from Clarke, a man who was not so squeamish in this regard. He ran to the top of the stairs and threw it down into the hall.

He pushed open the bathroom door, then the bedroom, and finally, the utility cupboard at the far end of the landing.

He returned to the sitting-room. Clarke was on his knees, one hand cuffed to the radiator, Presley standing over him, a handkerchief wrapped around his bloody fist.

Clarke was bleeding from the nose and groaning softly as he held his fingers to the watery, pale blisters that were his big scalds.

'Where are they?' asked Kavanagh. All friendliness had gone from his voice; he felt a cheat, a fraud, like someone who talks down a suicide and then imprisons him.

'She had my soul,' murmured Clarke through his bloodied teeth. 'I had to have it back.'

'Where *are* they?' repeated Kavanagh.

'I had to have it back,' mumbled Clarke.

Kavanagh rushed out of the door and down the stairs. He tried the handle of the shop door again. It didn't have the immovable feel of the door to the flat, but it wasn't going to give in to a shove. And, even if he had felt so inclined, the wire mesh on the door precluded his hurtling through the plate glass behind it.

Up the pavement, a hundred yards away, the road was under night repair. He sprinted towards the labourers, shouted, 'Police!' and took a pickaxe out of a man's hands.

The other labourers, orange plastic flashes on their donkey jackets, pursued the mad police impersonator up the road.

Kavanagh swung the axe at the door and wrenched and levered at the wire as the glass fell in. He smashed out the shards as the gathering crowd watched in disbelief from a safe distance.

The undercover sergeant had materialized and now stood behind him, punching the buttons of his phone and shouting into it for reinforcements.

Kavanagh stood alone in the silence of the shop.

Familiar smells of wood shavings and glue and polish. But something else, too. Stronger, more acrid, it caught in the throat and in the nose.

The policeman slowly approached the bath. There was a deal of bubbling, and there were pools and splashes all over the floor where the gallons of displaced liquid had washed over the side.

He took the smooth pole from the corner and touched the surface. The pole immediately made contact with something soft and giving.

24

Jeff Clarke sat opposite the inspector and smoked his cigarette. The spools of the cassette recorder whirred; the red
recording light glowed.

DI Frank Kavanagh had conducted many hundreds of
interviews during his twenty years in the police force.
He'd charged dozens of suspects with myriad crimes.

He'd sat opposite men (and a few women) who could
barely hold the stub of a pencil in their ungainly hands.
And watched others who wrote with the extravagant
hand that he always, now, associated with deceit.

He'd seen the repressed hand of sex offenders, forcing
out each word onto the lined paper, non-writing arm
crooked around their confessions, just as children at junior
school protected *their* work from others' eyes.

Since the sound recording of all interviews was made
mandatory, Kavanagh had sat opposite the tongue-tied
and the verbose, the prolix and the mute.

He'd recorded interviews with stammerers; with
fraudsters and embezzlers who had the panache of
government front-bench spokesmen; and with recidivist
felons who, accompanied by their stone-faced solicitors,
managed only two words: 'No comment.'

He'd listened to the 'prepared statement', beloved of
politicians and those who emerged from the Old Bailey,
case dismissed by a diffident jury, lay-people bamboozled
into confusion and doubt by wily defence counsel.

The 'prepared statement' always suggested to Kavanagh

a document compiled behind closed doors; words wrought with the due caution of the culpable.

Out they came, brazen beneath the media glare, impregnable behind the solitary sheet of flapping paper.

But say the truth a thousand times, a detail added here, one omitted there, it mattered little. Lie, and when that change *did* come, in that detail altered, the alibi began to collapse. In that first trickle the sea wall was breached.

It took time, of course; for hours, sometimes days, the waves of questioning were rebuffed by the defendant's obduracy.

But Kavanagh was a wave machine; and he knew the story of Canute.

Clarke was no charlatan. He was not sly or even evasive. No, he was none of these things.

He was slow to start because he was inhabiting his person, finding the 'voice'.

You didn't go on and play King Lear straight out of the pub, or Cymbeline fresh off the squash court. You sat alone, thought about your part.

The spools of the cassette whirred. 'I'm sorry,' he murmured.

Kavanagh spoke into the microphone: 'Questioning of Jeffrey Clarke, by Detective Inspector Francis Kavanagh, suspended at 11.20 a.m., Tuesday, the 9th November.'

The red light glowed. Kavanagh sat quietly, Presley at his side, the arresting officer in the corner.

After another ten minutes of silence, the man nodded his head and said, 'All right. Now.'

Kavanagh turned on the machine and announced the interview once more.

Clarke lifted his head slightly and began in a quiet voice.

'She left me, and it was more than I could bear. At first, I thought it would be all right. We'd talked about parting. Things weren't right any more: there had been the loss of the baby. But when she went, it was too . . . sudden.

183

'We had been married a long time. We had our daughter. And then she left. She told me about her affair at Open University, after all those years, when I thought it had been all right between us.

'It was like replaying the past. We had been through all that. In our past, long ago.

'What would she tell me next year? Or the year after that?

'There was no trust. There never could be. I had hurt her. Now she was hurting me back. And I knew she could go on doing it.

'She could always hurt me more. What could I believe? I pleaded with her to tell me everything, so that I could carry on, start again.

'I know there was more.

'I couldn't force her. I never have. You have to let people do what they want to do. Perhaps I shouldn't have, because it hurt me so much. And then I had to do what *I* did, to all of them.

'I have feelings. I *think* about things.

'After the news, I'm thinking about what has happened. It stays with me.'

Kavanagh wanted to ask: 'Is that why you killed six people? Because you're so sensitive?' He sat silently, said nothing, let the man talk.

'I tried to carry on. But it was going round and round in my head.

'I tried to live, but I couldn't. The whole thing became one endless agonized memory of the bad things in our life, and I knew that the only way I could make things right again would be to cut them away.'

There was a pause.

'Y^s?' said Kavanagh.

He looked directly at the inspector: 'I see pain on faces. A special kind of pain. A pain that only the sufferers know. I'd seen it before, but never recognized it, never knew it for what it was.

'It's a club, Inspector: the people who have been broken by loss. But you can only get in if you're a member. It's like those handshakes the Freemasons have. There's no mistaking it.

'You know, I even watch the football managers. Watch them being interviewed after the game. I watch their eyes, and they're talking about the second goal, but *I'm* looking at their eyes. And I can *tell*. I look at people in bars, and the people in the shops. And I can tell.

'We're a club. We know each other's pain; each other's special scent. It is some comfort. A little comfort.'

The man stubbed out his cigarette and looked back at Kavanagh. 'You know what I'm talking about, Inspector?'

'Go on,' said the policeman.

Clarke breathed very deeply, lit another cigarette. 'She had my soul. I had to have it back. I could die, I was not afraid of that, it would be a relief.

'But what if I died and was left in limbo, a wraith, ". . . confin'd to fast in fires"?

'You see, Inspector, my soul. You know, I had to have it back . . .'

'But why the others?' said Kavanagh. 'So long ago; why them? And why them *first*?'

'They were all involved, Inspector. I had to square it all. But her last, because you always go to the husband first. Prime suspect. You would have come straight to me. As it was, you were looking for me as soon as you made a connection between the three of them. But I knew it would take you a long time.

'It was hard enough for *me* to find them, and I knew who they were. They'd spread out, they were from different backgrounds, and it was all a long time ago.

'So, I started with Sugar.' He paused. 'I'm sorry about his wife. But I had other people to see to, and so I couldn't just leave her to come out and tell you. I had to kill her too.'

185

He looked up at Kavanagh. He seemed to expect the policeman to sanction the murder.

'She'd never done anything to me. But they *were* married. They should stay together.'

He appeared to be serious.

'And then it was John Lacey. All those years ago I used to like John. I think he liked me, too. I didn't even really blame him for being with Sarah that time. It wasn't *his* fault.

'But when she told me about it, years later, it was hard for me.

'I forgave her. Again. I think a man will forgive the woman he loves a lot. And I loved her, really.'

He went on seamlessly, his monologue a further purgation. 'I had a couple of affairs. But she didn't care. A bit, maybe. But she wasn't *crucified*. You know, I'm the one who remembers things.'

'Yes, you said,' said Kavanagh.

'The *Sunday Times*: "Life in the Day". Do you know that series?'

Kavanagh nodded. He always read it straight after the football results.

'There was a man who lived in a tree . . .'

Presley raised his eyebrows.

'Out in Wales somewhere, years ago,' continued Clarke. 'And I still wonder about him. Is he still there? In that tree?

'On TV once, there was a documentary: a man with a short-term memory, and every time his wife went out of the room to make a cup of tea, when she came back in, he greeted her as if they hadn't seen one another for years.'

Clarke smiled. 'It was beautiful. His wife found it exhausting. But I thought it was wonderful.

'And a man with tinnitus, that constant noise in his ears. I think about him, too. I can't *forget* these people. I should. But I can't.

'And there's me going round and round, like a hamster on a wheel: the noise in my ears is *our* past, not just some buzzing.

'Round and round on a loop of pain and memory.

'I moved away; eventually went abroad. I tried, I *really* tried. I took all the advice.

'But, do you know, the only time I felt all right, just for a while, was when I remembered the wrong that *I* had done *her*?

'I thought about the baby; our baby and her awful loss. And then I felt sorry for her. And then, I don't know why, I felt a bit better myself.

'But I couldn't make it last. How long can you go on like that, hurting yourself with memories of the past so that you can get through each day?

'I did do it, for days at a time. I would trick myself into that state, lead myself again into that hurt where I could feel guilt and sorrow, and then feel better.

'I even asked for her forgiveness; showed her my contrition. But she didn't write back. Not a word.'

'I'm not sure she got your letters,' interrupted Kavanagh. 'I think . . . after they moved away, she stopped receiving them.'

Clarke seemed not to hear. He carried on, 'I went to church and prayed. ''Forgive us our sins, as we forgive those that trespass against us . . .''

'I wanted to be like one of those people on TV, after their child is killed by a joyrider, or their family is blown up by a bomb, and they say they want to forgive the killers, and they will pray for them. I wanted to be like that.

'But I couldn't do it. I couldn't make it last; I couldn't get off the loop.

'I wrote the pain into my new book, tried to exorcize it in that way. But I knew what would happen when it was ended. I became afraid of finishing.

'The book didn't matter.' He paused and smiled. 'But I think it *was* good writing.

'What would I do with my dreams when I woke in the morning and didn't have my book to put them into?'

'And?' said Kavanagh.

'And the book was finished. I couldn't say any more. I sent it away. My time had come. *I* was going to start living in the moment. I was going to be the one who "kisses the joy as it flies . . ."

'It's what Briony had always told me to do.

'Sarah was with Burchell. They were together.

'I couldn't bear it. I didn't mind killing myself, but I was afraid that my death would be the same as my life, I had to kill my past first, recover my soul from her.

'I'd put it into the book. Now, I was going to *do* it. The pen; the sword. I don't believe that proverb.

'I felt better. I was getting free. Doing it would release me. Any price was cheap for my peace of mind. Anything to stop my pain.

'And now I *am* free. It's done, and I have peace again. I will be able to sleep at night again. I know I will.'

The inspector looked at him; he thought not of murder, or manslaughter. The word that came to his mind was no word: it was mans-*laughter*.

Kavanagh suspended the interview. He would question him in detail about the crimes later.

The policemen made to leave.

'Inspector?' said Clarke.

'Yes?' said Kavanagh.

'My daughter? Briony.'

'Yes,' said the inspector, looking into the man's eyes.

'Would it be possible for me to see her?'

The inspector continued to look at the man. But whatever it was that he looked for, he did not see.

'Yes,' said Kavanagh, 'of course.'

'Thank you,' said Clarke. 'She's all I've got now, you see.'

'Yes,' said the inspector.

The policemen walked down the corridor.

'Round the fuckin' bend,' said Presley. 'Make a space, Broadmoor, here we come.'

Kavanagh was silent.